ROB
Large Print   Roberts, Nora.

Song of the West.

$30.95

DATE			

Song of the West

*Also by Nora Roberts
in Large Print:*

Affaire Royale
Birthright
Chesapeake Blue
Dance Upon the Air
From This Day
Heaven and Earth
Island of Flowers
Lawless
Midnight Bayou
Night Moves
The Playboy Prince
Risky Business
Search for Love
This Magic Moment
Untamed
A Will and Way

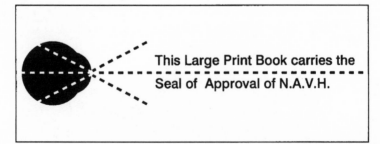

This Large Print Book carries the
Seal of Approval of N.A.V.H.

Song of the West

Nora Roberts

WHEELER
PUBLISHING

Published in 2004 by arrangement with Harlequin Books S.A.

Wheeler Large Print Romance.

The text of this Large Print edition is unabridged.
Other aspects of the book may vary from the original edition.

Set in 16 pt. Plantin by Christina S. Huff.

Printed in the United States on permanent paper.

Library of Congress Cataloging-in-Publication Data

Roberts, Nora.
    Song of the West / Nora Roberts.
      p. cm.
    ISBN 1-58724-697-X (lg. print : hc : alk. paper)
    1. Wyoming — Fiction. 2. Cowboys — Fiction. 3. Large type
books. I. Title.
PS3568.O243S66 2004
  813´.54—dc22
                                  2004052044

Song of the West

As the Founder/CEO of NAVH, the only national health agency solely devoted to those who, although not totally blind, have an eye disease which could lead to serious visual impairment, I am pleased to recognize Thorndike Press★ as one of the leading publishers in the large print field.

Founded in 1954 in San Francisco to prepare large print textbooks for partially seeing children, NAVH became the pioneer and standard setting agency in the preparation of large type.

Today, those publishers who meet our standards carry the prestigious "Seal of Approval" indicating high quality large print. We are delighted that Thorndike Press is one of the publishers whose titles meet these standards. We are also pleased to recognize the significant contribution Thorndike Press is making in this important and growing field.

Lorraine H. Marchi, L.H.D.
Founder/CEO
NAVH

★ Thorndike Press encompasses the following imprints: Thorndike, Wheeler, Walker and Large Pr int Press.

Chapter 1

The land in southeast Wyoming is a magnificent paradox. Spreading plains and rolling hills co-exist with rocky mountains and thick velvet pines. From the kitchen window, the view was astounding, and Samantha Evans halted in her duties for a moment to drink it in.

The Rockies dominated the vast curtain of sky, their peaks laced with snow, though it was late March.

Samantha wondered if she would still be in Wyoming the following winter. She dreamed of long walks with the air biting and sharp on her cheeks, or wild rides on a spirited mount with hooves kicking up a flurry of white. But none of that could happen until her sister was well enough to be left alone.

A frown creased her smooth brow. Sabrina was her reason for being in Wyoming, with its majestic mountains and quiet plains, rather than in the more familiar surroundings of Philadelphia's tall buildings and traffic-choked streets.

The two sisters had always been close, with that special, magical intimacy that twins share. They were not identical. Though they were the same in height and build, Samantha's eyes were a dark cornflower blue, widely set, with thick, spiky lashes, while Sabrina's eyes were a light gray. Both faces were oval set with small, straight noses and well-shaped mouths, but while Samantha's rich brown hair, with its highlights of gold, was shoulder length with a fringe of bangs, Sabrina's ash blonde was short, framing her face with delicate curls. The bond between them was strong and enduring. Even when Sabrina had married Dan Lomax and moved so many miles away to settle on his ranch in the Laramie Basin, their devotion had remained constant and unwavering.

They kept in touch by phone and letter, which helped to mitigate Samantha's aching loneliness. And she was happy in her sister's delight in the coming baby. The two women had laughed and planned together over the phone. But that was before Dan's call. Samantha had been aroused from a deep predawn sleep by the shrill ringing of the phone. She reached groggily for it, but was instantly alerted by the anxious tone of her brother-in-law's voice. "Sam," he said without any preamble, "Bree's been very ill. We did manage to save the baby, but she has to be very careful for a while now. She will have to stay in bed and have constant round-the-clock care. We are trying to find someone to —"

Samantha had only one thought — her sister, the person she loved best in the world. "Don't worry, Dan, I will come immediately."

She was on the plane to Wyoming less than twenty-four hours later. . . .

The whistle of the kettle brought Samantha back to the present. She began to brew the herbal tea, placing delicate floral cups on a silver tray.

"Teatime," she called as she entered the living room. Sabrina was propped up with pillows and comforters on the long wood-edged sofa. Though her smile was warm, her cheeks still retained a delicate pallor.

"Just like the movies," Sabrina commented as her sister set a tray on the pine table. "But the role of Camille is getting to be a bore."

"I imagine so." Samantha poured the fragrant tea into cups. "But you may as well get used to it, Bree, you've got the part for a month's run." She transferred a large gray striped cat from Sabrina's lap to her own, offered Sabrina a steaming cup and sat on the rug. "Has Shylock been keeping you company?"

"He's a terrible snob." With a wry smile, Sabrina sipped at her tea. "He did graciously allow me to scratch his ears. I have to admit, I'm glad you brought him with you, he's my biggest entertainment." She sighed and lay back against the pillows, regarding her sister seriously. "I'm ashamed to be lying here feeling sorry for myself. I'm lucky." She rested her hand on her stomach in a protective gesture. "I shall have my baby, and I sit here moaning about your waiting on me."

"You're entitled to moan a bit, Bree," said Samantha, immediately sympathetic. "You're used to being active and busy."

"I've no right to complain. You gave up your job and left home to come out here and take care of me." Another deep sigh escaped, and her gray eyes were dangerously moist. "If Dan had told me what you were planning to do, I would never have allowed it."

"You couldn't have stopped me." Samantha attempted to lighten the mood. "That's what older sisters are for."

"You never forget those seven minutes, do you?" Sabrina's eyes cleared, and a reluctant smile curved her generous mouth.

"Nope, it gives me seniority."

"But your job, Sam."

"Don't worry." Samantha made another dismissive gesture. "I'll get another job in the fall. There's more than one high school in the country, and they all have gym teachers. Besides, I needed a vacation."

"Vacation!" Sabrina exclaimed. "Cleaning, cooking, caring for an invalid. You call that a vacation?"

"My dear Sabrina, have you ever tried to teach an overweight, totally uncoordinated teenager the intricacies of the parallel bars? Well, the stories I could tell you about vacations."

10

"Sam, what a pair we are. You with your teen-agers and me with my preadolescent Mozarts. Lord knows how many times I cleaned peanut butter off the keys of that old Wurlitzer before Dan came along and took me away from scales and infant prodigies. Do you think Mom expected us to come to this when she dragged us to all those lessons?"

"Ah, but we're well-rounded." Samantha's grin was faintly wicked. "Aren't you grateful? She always told us we'd be grateful one day for the ballet and the piano lessons."

"The voice lessons and the riding lessons," Sabrina continued, ticking them off on her fingers.

"Gymnastics and swimming lessons," Sabrina concluded with a giggle.

"Poor Mom." Samantha shifted Shylock to a more comfortable position. "I think she expected one of us to marry the president, and she wanted us to be prepared."

"We shouldn't make fun." Sabrina wiped her eyes with a tissue. "The lessons did give us our living."

"True. And I can still whip up a mean spinach soufflé."

"Ugh." Sabrina grimaced, and Samantha lifted her brows.

"Exactly."

"You have your medals," Sabrina reminded her. Her smile warmed with pride and a trace of awe.

"Yes, I have the medals and the memories. Sometimes, it feels like yesterday instead of nearly ten years ago."

Sabrina smiled. "I can still remember my terrified excitement when you first swung onto the uneven bars. Even though I'd watched the routine countless times, I couldn't quite believe it was you. When they put that first Olympic medal around your neck, it was one of the happiest moments of my life."

"I remember thinking just before that competition, after I'd botched the balance beam so badly, that I couldn't do it. My legs felt like petroleum jelly, and I was mortally afraid I was going to be sick and disgrace myself. Then I saw Mom in the stands, and it ran through my mind how much she'd sacrificed. Not the money. The bending of those rather strange values of hers to allow me those years of training and those few heady moments of competition. I had to prove it was justified, I had to pay her back with something, even though I knew she'd never be able to say she was proud of me."

"You proved it was justified." Sabrina gave her twin a soft smile. "Even if you hadn't won on the bars and the floor exercises, you'd proved it by just being there. And she was proud of you, even if she didn't say it."

"You've always understood. So get over the idea I'm doing you a favor coming here. I want to be here. I *belong* here."

"Sam." Sabrina held out a hand. "I don't

know what I'd do without you. I don't know what I *ever* would have done without you."

"You'd manage," Samantha returned, giving the frail hand a squeeze. "You have Dan."

"Yeah, I do." The smile became soft. "This is the time of day that I miss him most. He should be home soon." Her gaze wandered to the glass-domed anniversary clock on the mantel above the fire.

"He said something about checking fences today. I can't quite get away from the image of him chasing rustlers or fighting off renegade Indians."

With a light laugh, Sabrina settled back among the cushions. "City slicker. You know, Sam, sometimes I can't even remember what Philadelphia looks like. Jake Tanner was riding along with Dan today to make sure the boundary fences were in good repair."

"Jake Tanner?" Samantha's question was idle.

"Oh, that's right, you haven't met him yet. The northwest corner of the ranch borders his. Of course, the Lazy L would fit into one corner of his ranch. He owns half the county."

"Ah, a land baron," Samantha concluded.

"A very apt description," Sabrina agreed. "The Double T, his ranch, is the most impressive I've seen. He runs it like clockwork, super efficient. Dan says he's not only an incredible rancher, but a very crafty businessman."

"Sounds like a bore," Samantha commented, wrinkling her nose. "Steel-gray hair around a

13

leathered face, a handlebar mustache drooping over his mouth and a generous belly hanging over his belt . . ."

Sabrina's laughter rang out, high and sweet.

"You're about as far off the mark as you can get. Jake Tanner is anything but a bore, and speaking from the safety of marital bliss, he's a fascinating man to look at. And, being rich, successful and unattached, all the females under forty buzz around him like bees around honey."

"Sounds like a good catch," Samantha said dryly. "Mom would love him."

"Absolutely," Sabrina agreed. "But Jake has eluded capture so far. Though from what Dan says, he does enjoy the chase."

"Now he sounds like a conceited bore." Samantha tickled Shylock's smooth belly.

"You can hardly blame him for taking what's offered." Sabrina defended the absent Jake Tanner with a vague movement of her shoulders. "I imagine he'll settle down soon. Lesley Marshall — her father's ranch borders the other side of the Double T — has her sights set on him. She's a very determined woman, as well as being more than a little spoiled, and dreadfully rich."

"Sounds like a perfect match."

"Mmm, maybe," Sabrina murmured. Her face creased in a small frown. "Lesley's nice enough when it suits her, and it's about time Jake had a wife and family. I'm fond of Jake. I'd like to see him set up with someone with more warmth."

14

"Listen to the old married woman." Samantha addressed a dozing and unconcerned Shylock. "A year of nuptial bliss, and she can't stand to see anyone unattached."

"True. I'm going to start on you next."

"Thanks for the warning."

"Wyoming's full of good-looking cowboys and handsome ranchers." Sabrina continued to smile as her sister grimaced. "You could find a worse place to settle down."

"I have no objection to settling here, Bree. I've become quite attached to the wide open spaces. But —" she paused significantly "— cowboys and ranchers are not among my immediate plans for the future." She rose from the floor in a fluid motion. "I've got to check on that roast. Here." She handed her sister the novel that rested on the table. "Read your love stories, you incurable romantic."

"You won't be so cynical when you fall in love," Sabrina predicted with the wisdom of experience.

"Sure." Samantha's grin was indulgent.

"There'll be bells ringing and fireworks shooting and trumpets blaring." She patted her sister's hand and strolled from the room, calling over her shoulder. "Angels singing, flames leaping . . ."

"Just you wait," Sabrina shouted after her.

Samantha busied herself preparing vegetables for the evening meal, clucking her tongue at her sister's nonsense. *Love,* she sniffed derisively. Her only experience with that complex emotion had been fending off unwanted attentions from eager males. Not once had any man lit an answering spark in her. But whatever this love was, it worked for Bree. The younger twin had always been more delicate, softer and more dependent. And though Sabrina was trying to be brave and strong, her sister knew the fear of miscarriage still lurked in the back of her mind. She needed Dan's support and love, and right now, she needed to feel his arms around her.

Like the answer to a prayer, Samantha spotted two figures on horseback approaching from the lower pasture. Grabbing her heavy jacket from the hook by the back door, she scurried out of the kitchen and into the cold March air.

As Dan and his companion drew closer, Samantha greeted him with a smile and a wave. She had noticed, even at a distance, Dan's expression of concern. But a smile relaxed his features when he spotted Samantha.

"Sabrina's all right?" he asked as he reined in next to her.

"She's fine," Samantha assured him. "Just a trifle restless, and tremendously lonely for her husband."

"Did she eat better today?"

Samantha's smile warmed, lighting her face with a quick flash of astonishing beauty.

"Her appetite was much better. She's trying

16

very hard." Samantha lifted a hand to stroke the smooth flank of the gelding he rode. "What she needs now is you."

"I'll be in as soon as I stable my horse."

"Oh, Dan, for heaven's sake. Let your hand do it, or I'll do it myself. Bree needs you."

"But . . ."

" 'S all right, boss," the other horseman interrupted, and Samantha spared him a brief glance. "I'll tend to your horse. You go on and see the missus."

Dan flashed his companion a wide grin and dismounted. "Thanks," he said simply as he handed over the reins and turned to Samantha. "Coming in?"

"No." She shook her head and hunched her shoulders in the confines of her jacket. "You two could use some time alone, and I'd like some air."

"Thanks, Sam." He pinched her cheek with brotherly affection and moved off toward the house.

Waiting until the door closed behind him, Samantha walked over and dropped wearily onto the stump used for splitting wood. Resting her back against the fence, she breathed deeply, devouring the brisk, cold air. The strain of caring for her sister in addition to running the house and cooking the meals, including, over his objection, Dan's predawn breakfast, had taken its toll.

"A few more days," she whispered as she

closed her eyes. "A few more days and I'll have adjusted to the routine and feel more like myself." The heavy corded jacket insulated her from the bite of the cold, and she tilted back her head, allowing the air to play on her cheeks as her mind drifted on the edge of exhaustion.

"Funny place to take a nap."

Samantha sat up with a jerk, confused and disoriented by sleep. Her eyes traveled up to the speaker's face. It was a lean face, skin bronzed by the sun and stretched tightly over cheekbones, all lines and shadows, hollows and angles. The eyes were arresting, deep-set and heavily lashed. But it was their color, a deep, pure jade that caught and held her attention. His dusky gold hair curled from under a well-battered Stetson.

"Evening, ma'am." Though he touched the brim of his hat with due respect, his extraordinary eyes were faintly mocking.

"Good evening," she returned, struggling for dignity.

"Person could catch a bad chill sitting out too long after the sun's low. Wind's picking up, too." His speech was slow and thickly drawled. His weight was distributed evenly on both legs, hands deep in pockets. "Oughtn't to be out without a hat." His comment was accompanied by a fractional movement of his head toward her unadorned one. "Hat helps keep the heat in."

"I'm not cold." She feared for a moment her

18

teeth would chatter and betray her. "I was . . . I was just getting some air."

"Yes, ma'am." He nodded in agreement, glancing behind her at the last, dying brilliance of sun as it slipped behind circling peaks. "Fine evening for setting out and watching the sunset."

Her eyes flashed at the teasing. She was embarrassed to have been caught sleeping. He smiled a slow, careless smile that crept unhurried across his face. The movement of his lips caused the hollows to deepen, the shadows to shift. Unable to resist, Samantha's lips curved in response.

"All right, I confess. You caught me napping. I don't suppose you'd believe I was just resting my eyes."

"No, ma'am." His answer was grave, with just a hint of apology.

"Well." She rose from her seat and was dismayed at how far she still had to look up to meet his eyes. "If you keep quiet about it, I'll see to it that you get a piece of the apple pie I baked for dinner."

"That's a mighty tempting offer." He considered it with a long-fingered hand reaching up to stroke his chin. "I'm partial to apple pie. Only one or two things I'm more partial to." His eyes roamed over her in a thorough and intense study that caused her heart to pound with unaccustomed speed.

There was something different about this

man, she thought swiftly, something unique, a vitality at odds with lazy words and careless smiles. He pushed his hat back farther on his head, revealing more disorderly curls. "You've got yourself a deal." He held out his hand to confirm the agreement, and she placed her small hand in his.

"Thanks." The single word was breathless, as she found her speech hampered by the currents running up her arm. Abruptly, she pulled her hand away, wondering what it was about him which disturbed her equilibrium. "I'm sorry if I was short before, about Dan's horse." She spoke now in a rush, to conceal a reaction she could not understand.

"No need to apologize," he assured her, and the new soft texture in his tone both warmed and unnerved her. "We're all fond of Mrs. Lomax."

"Yes, well, I . . ." she stammered, suddenly needing to put a safe distance between herself and this slow-talking man. "I'd better go inside. Dan must be hungry." She looked past him and spotted his horse, still saddled, waiting patiently. "You didn't stable your horse. Aren't you finished for the day?" Hearing the concern in her own voice, she marveled at it. Really, she thought, annoyed, why should I care?

"Oh, yes, ma'am, I'm finished." There was laughter in his voice now, but Samantha failed to notice. She began to study the mount with care.

It was a magnificent animal, dark, gleaming chestnut, at least sixteen hands, she estimated, classic lines, fully flowing mane and proud, dished face. Arabian. Samantha knew horses and she recognized a full-blooded Arabian stallion when she saw one. What in the world . . . ? "That's an Arabian." Her words interrupted her thoughts.

"Yes, ma'am," he agreed easily, entirely too easily. Her eyes narrowed with suspicion as she turned to him.

"No ranch hand is going to be riding around on a horse that's worth six months' pay." She stared at him and he returned the steady survey with a bland, poker face. "Who are you?"

"Jake Tanner, ma'am." The slow grin appeared again, widening, deepening, then settling as he lifted the brim of his hat at the introduction. "Pleased to meet you."

The land baron with the women at his feet, Samantha's brain flashed. Anger darkened her eyes.

"Why didn't you say so?"

"Just did," he pointed out.

"Oh." She tossed back her thick fall of hair. "You know very well what I mean. I thought you were one of Dan's men."

"Yes, ma'am." He nodded.

"Stop *ma'aming* me," she commanded. "What a mean trick! All you had to do was open your mouth and say who you were. I would have stabled Dan's horse myself."

21

"I didn't mind." His expression became annoyingly agreeable. "It wasn't any trouble, and you had a nice rest."

"Well, Mr. Tanner, you had a fine laugh at my expense. I hope you enjoyed it," she said coldly.

"Yes, ma'am." The grin widened without seeming to move at all. "I did."

"I told you to stop . . ." She halted, biting her lip with frustration. "Oh, forget it." Tossing her head, she took a few steps toward the house, then turned back crossly. "I notice your accent has modified quite a bit, Mr. Tanner."

He did not reply, but continued to stand negligently, his hands in his pockets, his face darkened by the late-afternoon shadows. Samantha spun back around and stomped toward the house.

"Hey," he called out, and she turned toward him before she could halt the reflex. "Do I still get that pie?"

She answered his question with a glare. His laughter, deep and rich, followed her into the house.

Chapter 2

The sound of the slamming door reverberated through the ranch house as Samantha struggled out of her jacket and marched into the living room. At the sight of her sister's face Sabrina slipped down into the pillows, picked up the novel lying on her lap and buried her nose in its pages. Dan, however, did not recognize the storm warning in his sister-in-law's blue eyes and flushed cheeks. He greeted her with a friendly, ingenuous smile.

"Where's Jake?" His gaze slid past her. "Don't tell me he went home without a cup of coffee?"

"He can go straight to the devil without his coffee."

"I expect he wanted to get home before dark," Dan concluded. His nod was sober, but his eyes were brilliant with merriment.

"Don't play innocent with me, Dan Lomax." Samantha advanced on him. "That was a rotten trick, letting me think he was one of your hands, and . . ." A giggle escaped from behind the paperback. "I'm glad you think it's amusing that your sister's been made a fool of."

"Oh, Sam, I'm sorry." Warily, Sabrina lowered the book. "It's just hard to believe anyone could mistake Jake Tanner for a ranch hand." She burst out laughing, and Samantha was torn between the pleasure of seeing her sister laugh and irritation at being the brunt of the joke.

"Well, really, what makes him so special?" she demanded. "He dresses like every other cowboy I've seen around here, and that hat of his has certainly seen better days." But, she remembered, there *had* been something special about him that she had not quite been able to define. She firmly dismissed this disquieting thought. "The nerve of him." She rounded on Dan again. "Calling you boss, and ma'aming me in that exaggerated drawl."

"Reckon he was just being polite," Dan suggested. His smile was amiable and pure. Samantha sent him the look that terrified her students.

"Men." Raising her eyes, she searched the ceiling in hopes of finding the answer there. "You're all alike, and you all stick together." She bent and scooped up the sleeping Shylock and marched into the kitchen.

Time at the ranch passed quickly. Though her days were full and busy, Samantha fretted for some of the physical outlet that had so long been part of her life. At times, the confinement

24

of the house was suffocating. Years of training and discipline had left her with an inherent need for activity.

Unconsciously, she separated her life into three categories: the pre-Olympic years, the Olympic years and the post-Olympic years.

The pre-Olympic years were a blur of lessons, piano teachers, dance instructors, her mother's gentle but inescapable admonishments to "be a lady." Then, the first time she had gripped the lower bar of the unevens, the new chapter had begun.

By the time she was twelve years old, she had remarkable promise. The gymnastics instructor had informed her mother, who was more distressed than pleased at the praise. Though her mother had objected to more intense training, Samantha had ultimately prevailed.

The hours of training became months, county meets became state meets, and national competitions became international competitions. When Samantha was picked for the Olympic team, it was just another step down a road she was determined to follow. Weariness and aching muscles were accepted without hesitation.

Then it was over, and at fifteen she had found it necessary to alter what had become a way of life. College had to be considered, and earning a living. The years passed into the post-Olympic period, and she remembered her days of athletic competitions as a dream. Now her life was shifting again, though she was unsure as to the direction. The mountains and plains were calling to her, inviting her to explore, but she buried her desires, remaining indoors to see to her sister's needs. Dan is a busy man, she thought as she prepared lunch, and Bree needs someone within calling distance during this critical period. When she's better, there will be plenty of time to see the country.

She arched her back and rubbed a small spot of tension at the base of her neck. The kitchen door opened and Dan burst in, accompanied by Jake Tanner. Samantha met the amused green eyes levelly, though once more she felt treacherously at a disadvantage.

Her hair had been carelessly scooped on the top of her head that morning, and now, with their usual abandonment, stray locks were beginning to escape confinement. She was dressed in a black ribbed sweater that had seen too many washings and ancient jeans, splattered, faded, patched and too tight. She resisted the urge to raise her hand to her tumbling hair, forced a smile and turned to her brother-in-law.

"Hello, Dan. What are you doing home this time of day?" Purposefully, she ignored the tall figure beside him.

"Wasn't too far out," Dan explained. Slipping off his jacket and hat, he tossed both over the hooks provided. "Jake was giving me a hand, so I figured it was only neighborly to bring him back for lunch."

"Hope I'm not imposing, ma'am." The slow smile spread, once more rearranging the angles of his face.

"No imposition, Mr. Tanner. But you'll have to settle for potluck."

"My favorite dish —" he paused, giving her a cheeky wink "— next to apple pie."

Samantha sent him a withering glance and turned away to warm the previous evening's stew.

"I'll just go tell Sabrina I'm home," Dan announced to the room in general, and strode away. Samantha did her best to ignore Jake's disturbing presence. She stirred the stew busily.

"Smells good." Jake moved over to the stove and lounged against it. Samantha went to the cupboard to get the bowls.

When she turned back to place them on the round kitchen table, she noticed that he had shed his outdoor clothing. The slim-fitting jeans, snug and low on narrow hips, accentuated his leanness. His flannel shirt fitted over his broad shoulders and hard chest before tapering down to a narrow waist. The athlete in her immediately responded to the firm, well-proportioned body; there was not an ounce of spare flesh on him.

"Don't talk much, do you?" The drawl was there again, the exaggerated twang of the previous evening. Samantha turned her head, prepared to freeze him with her eyes.

His face was barely inches from hers as he

27

slouched by the stove. For a moment, her mind ceased to function.

"I really have nothing to say to you, Mr. Tanner." She struggled to keep her voice cold and detached, but she could feel the blood rush to her face.

"Well, now, we'll have to see if we can change that." He spoke with easy confidence as he straightened to his full height. "We're not much on formalities around here. Just make it Jake." Though his words were spoken with his usual lazy delivery, there was an undertone of command. Samantha's chin rose in defense.

"Maybe I prefer to keep things formal between us, Mr. Tanner."

His lips were curved in his careless smile, but in his eyes she now recognized that special something that separated him from an ordinary ranch hand. *Power.* She wondered how she had missed it at their first meeting.

"I don't think there's much chance of that." He paused and tugged at a loose lock of his hair before adding with irritating emphasis, "Ma'am. Nope, I don't think there's much chance of that at all."

Samantha was saved from coming up with a suitable rebuttal by Dan's reappearance. She began to spoon the stew into ceramic bowls, noting to her dismay that her hands were not altogether steady. This man was infuriating her with his arrogantly lazy confidence. I have never met a more irritating male, she thought. He

28

thinks he can switch on that rugged cowboy charm and women will drop in droves at his feet. Well, maybe some do, but not this one.

"Okay, Sam?" Dan's voice shattered the electric silence.

"What? I'm sorry, I wasn't listening."

"You'll keep Jake company over lunch, won't you? I'll have mine in the living room with Sabrina."

She swore silently. "Of course," she answered with an impersonal smile.

Within a short time, Samantha found herself sitting across from the man she wanted most to avoid.

"You've a fine hand with dumplings, Sam." Her brows rose involuntarily at his easy use of her nickname, but she kept her voice even.

"Thank you, Mr. Tanner. It's just one of my many talents."

"I'm sure it is," he agreed with an inclination of his head.

"You haven't changed much from the girl in the picture in Sabrina's parlor." Samantha was astonished.

"You'd have been about fifteen," he continued. "A bit skinnier than you are now, but your hair was the same, not quite willing to stay bundled on top of your head." Samantha's blank expression had turned to a frown at the word skinnier. She remembered the photo clearly.

"You'd just finished winning your second

29

medal." She had indeed been fifteen. The picture had been snapped at the moment she had completed her floor routine. It had captured the look of stunned triumph, for she had known in that instant that a medal was hers.

"Sabrina's just about as proud of you as you are worried about her." Samantha said nothing, only staring into the lean, handsome features. His brows rose ever so slightly, a movement that would have gone unnoticed had she not been so intent on his face. For a moment, she forgot the thread of the conversation, caught up suddenly in a series of small, irrelevant details: the curling gold which spilled over his brow, the tiny white scar on his jawline, the thickness of his long lashes. Confused, she dropped her eyes to her bowl and struggled to bring her thoughts to order.

"I'd forgotten Bree had that picture," she said. "It was a long time ago."

"So now you teach. You don't look like any gym teacher I ever knew."

"Oh, really?"

"No, ma'am." He shook his head slowly and considered her through another mouthful of stew. "Don't look strong enough or old enough."

"I assure you, Jake, I'm both strong enough and old enough for my profession."

"What made you become a gym teacher?" His sudden question caught her off balance, and she stared at him.

30

"Well, I . . ." Her shoulders moved restlessly. "Our mother was a fanatic on lessons when Bree and I were growing up." She smiled in spite of herself. "We took lessons in everything, Mom's theory on being well-rounded. Anyway, Bree found her talent in music and I developed a knack for the physical. For a while, I focused on gymnastics, then, when the time came to work, it seemed natural. Bree taught little people to play the classics, and I teach bigger people to tumble."

"Do you like your work? Are you happy with it?"

"As a matter of fact, I do," she retorted. "I like the activity, I like being involved in a physical type of work. It can be frustrating at times, of course. Some of the girls I teach would rather be flirting with their boyfriends than learning gymnastics, I suspect."

"And you yourself are more interested in calisthenics than men?" The question was delivered with a broad masculine smile.

"That's hardly relevant," she snapped, annoyed that she had lowered her guard.

"You don't think so?"

Samantha scraped back her chair and moved to the stove. "Coffee?"

"Yes, ma'am, black." It was unnecessary to turn around; she felt the slow grin crease his face as clearly as if she had witnessed it with her eyes. She set the cup down on the table with a bang. Before she could spin back to pour her

31

own, her hand was captured in a firm grip. There was nothing soft about the hand. It was hard and masculine.

Completely outmatched in the short battle that ensued, Samantha discovered that under the lean, lanky exterior lay an amazing strength. Deciding that it was undignified to grapple in her sister's kitchen, she allowed her hand to rest quietly in his, meeting his laughing eyes with a resentful glare. Her heart began to pound uncomfortably against her ribs.

"What do you want?" Her voice came out in a husky whisper. His eyes left hers to travel slowly down to the generous curve of her mouth, lingering until she could taste the heat on her lips, as real as a kiss. Taking his time, he moved his gaze back to her eyes.

"You're jumpy." His observation was laconic, as if none of the heat had touched him, though she herself was beginning to suffocate. "Powerful strong for such a little bit of a thing."

"I'm not little," she retorted. "You're just so big." She began to tug at her hand again, feeling a near desperate urgency to shake off the contact that was infusing her with an unexplained weakness around the knees.

"Your eyes are fabulous when you're angry, Sam." His tone was conversational. "Temper agrees with you. You grow beautiful with it." He laughed and pulled her closer.

"You're insufferable," she said, still struggling to escape his grasp.

"For telling you you're beautiful? I was just stating the obvious. I'm sure it's been mentioned to you once or twice before."

"You men are all the same." She ceased her struggles long enough to aim a lethal glare. "Always grabbing and groping."

"I don't grope, Samantha." His drawl was feather-soft. For an instant, the cocky cowboy vanished, and she glimpsed the man, shrewd and ruthless, beneath. Here was a man who not only expected to have his own way, but would. "And the next time I grab you, it won't only be to hold your hand." Releasing her, he leaned back in his chair. "You have been warned."

Later, as Sabrina napped and the house grew still around her, Samantha found herself staring blankly at the pages of a novel. Scowling, she tossed it aside and rose from the sofa to pace to the window. What an infuriating man. Obviously, he considers himself irresistible. She began to wander the room, attempting to block out the effect his blatant virility had had on her.

It was too bad, she decided on her fourth circle, that all those good looks, all that strength and appeal, had to belong to such a rude, arrogant man.

Deciding that a brisk walk was just what she needed to get Jake Tanner out of her mind, she stopped her pacing and grabbed a warm jacket. Moments later she was out the door, gazing around her in delight at the beauty of the starlit

Wyoming night. Her breath puffed out in thin white mists as she moved. The air, tinged with frost, carried the aroma of pine, and she drank it in greedily, enjoying the mixed scent of hay and horses and aged wood. She could hear the lonely sound of a coyote calling to the full silver moon. And suddenly she realized that she had fallen in love with Wyoming. The spell of the mountains and plains was on her, and she was inexplicably glad she had come.

"Goodness, you were out a long time," her sister commented as Samantha plopped down in a wing-backed chair in front of the fire a few minutes later. "You must be frozen."

"No." Samantha stretched out her legs and sighed. "I love it out there. It's fantastic! I never realized how big the sky was before, and I don't think I'll ever get used to the space, the openness."

She turned her attention to the powerfully built man sitting next to her sister on her sofa. "I wonder if you appreciate it, Dan, living here all of your life. Even your letters, Bree, didn't do justice to that world out there." Running her fingers through her hair, she made a small sound of pleasure. "To someone used to traffic-choked streets and huge buildings, all this . . ." Her hands moved in an inadequate gesture.

"You haven't had much of a chance to see anything since you've been here," Dan observed. "You've been with us a month and you haven't gone a quarter mile away from the house. And that's been mostly to fetch the mail in the mornings."

"I'll have plenty of time to explore later. I'll be around through the summer."

"Just the same, we're not having you tied to the house while you're here, Sam," Dan announced, and sat back against the cushions. "Even the most devoted sister is entitled to a day off."

"Don't be silly. You make it sound as though I were slaving from dawn to dusk. Half the time I'm not doing anything."

"We know how hard you're working, Sam," Sabrina said quietly, glancing up at Dan before returning her gaze to her twin. "And I know the lack of activity is harder on you than the work. I also know how you disrupted your life to come out here and take care of me."

"Oh, Bree, for heaven's sake," Samantha began, shifting uncomfortably. "I never would have found out how much I love Wyoming if I hadn't come."

"Don't try to shrug if off, Sam." Dan grinned at the embarrassed motion of her shoulders. "We're grateful, and you'll just have to get used to us telling you so. But tomorrow, we're going to show we're grateful instead of just talking about it. We're kicking you out for the day."

"Huh?" Blankly, Sam blinked at the bland smile before shifting her gaze to Sabrina's serene one.

"That's right." His grin widened as she drew her brows together. "Tomorrow's Sunday, and I'm staying home with my wife. And you . . ." He pointed a warning finger at his sister-in-law. "You're going to have your pick of the horses and take off."

Samantha sprung up from her slouched position. "Do you mean it?" Her face was glowing with pleasure, and Dan's smile warmed with affection.

"Yes, little sister, I mean it. It should be more."

"The dapple-gray gelding," she began in a rush, ignoring the last part of his comment. "Can I take him?"

"Already inspected the stock, and it appears you know your horses." Dan chuckled and shook his head. "Spook's a good mount. A little frisky, but from what Sabrina's told me, you can handle him."

"Oh, I can, and I promise I'll be careful with him." She sprang from her chair and crossed the room, flinging her arms around his neck. "Thanks, Dan. You are absolutely my favorite brother-in-law, bar none."

"I think she likes the idea, Sabrina," Dan commented as he met his wife's eyes over Samantha's head. "In fact, I'd say she's downright pleased about it."

"And I thought I hid my emotions so effectively." She gave his cheek a loud, smacking kiss.

"You be ready to start out about nine." He

patted Samantha's slim shoulder. "Jake'll be around, then."

"Jake?" Samantha repeated. Her smile froze.

"Yeah, he'll be riding out with you. Actually," Dan continued, "he suggested the idea this afternoon. He thought it would do you good to get out of the house for a while." He sighed and scratched his dark head, managing to appear sheepish, for all his size. "I'm ashamed I didn't think of it first. I guess I've been a bit preoccupied and didn't notice you were looking a littled tired and hemmed in."

"I'm not tired," she denied automatically.

"Hemmed in?" Sabrina offered with a knowing smile.

"A little, maybe, but I'm hardly in the last stages of cabin fever. I'm sure it's very kind of Mr. Tanner to be so concerned about my welfare." She managed to say his name in a normal voice. "But there's certainly no need for him to go with me. I know he has hundreds of more important things to do with his Sunday."

"Well, now, he didn't seem to think so," Dan said. "It was his suggestion, and he seemed keen on the idea, too."

"I don't know why he would be," she muttered. "Besides, I don't want to impose on him. We're practically strangers. I can just go by myself."

"Nonsense." Dan's refusal was good-natured but firm. "I couldn't possibly let you ride out by yourself just yet, no matter how good you are on a horse. You don't know the country, and it's easy to get lost. There's always the possibility of an accident. Besides," he added, and his grin was expansive, "you're part of the family, and I grew up with Jake, so you're not strangers. If anyone knows his way around this part of Wyoming, he does." He shrugged and rested his back against the cushions. "He owns half of it, anyway." Samantha glanced at her sister for help. Sabrina, however, appeared to be engrossed in her needlepoint.

Frowning at the lack of support, Samantha stewed over her predicament. If she refused Jake's company, she would not only forfeit the opportunity to ride the Wyoming countryside, but she would spoil Sabrina's and Dan's plans for a day alone together. She shrugged in resignation and offered a smile.

"I'll be ready at nine." She added to herself, If Jake Tanner can stand a day in my company, I guess I can stand a day in his.

Chapter 3

Sunday dawned with a sky as cold and clear as sapphire. The sun offered thin light and little warmth. To her annoyance, Samantha had overslept. Hurriedly, she showered and dressed in forest-green cords and a chunky beige pullover.

Her riding boots clattered on the parquet floor as she hurried from her room and down the hall to the kitchen. She frowned as she reached the doorway. Jake was sitting at the table, enjoying a cup of coffee with the air of one very much at home.

He was, she noted with illogical irritation, every bit as attractive as she remembered.

"Oh, you're here." Her greeting was hardly welcoming, but he returned it with his slow smile.

"Morning, ma'am."

"Don't start ma'aming me again," she said.

He remained silent as she clattered the cups in the cupboard and filled one with the steaming liquid from the pot on the stove.

"Sorry." She popped a piece of bread in the

toaster and turned to offer a peace-offering smile. "My! I overslept. I hope you haven't been waiting long."

"I've got all day," he answered, leaning back in his chair as if to emphasize his words.

She drew a slab of bacon and a carton of eggs from the refrigerator. "Have you eaten?" she asked in invitation.

"Yeah, thanks." He rose, poured himself another cup of coffee and resumed his position at the table. "Dan's already seen to breakfast for himself and Sabrina. They're having it in their room."

"Oh." She replaced the items and pulled out the butter.

"Aren't you going to eat?"

"Toast and coffee. I'm not much on breakfast."

"If you always eat like that," he observed over the rim of his cup, "it's no wonder you never grew any bigger."

"For goodness' sake." She whirled around, brandishing the butter knife. "I'm hardly a midget. I'm five-four, that's tall enough for anybody."

He held up his hands in mock surrender. "I never argue with an armed woman."

"Ready?" He rose when she had finished both the toast and another cup of coffee.

When she mumbled her assent, he plucked her jacket from its hook, holding it out so that she had no choice but to allow him to help her into it. She stiffened as his hands touched her shoulders and turned her to face him. Her pulses responded immediately. As if he were aware of her reaction, he began to do up her leather buttons with slow care. She jerked back, but his hold on the front of her coat prevented her from a clean escape.

"You're a pretty little thing," he drawled, completing his task with his eyes directly on hers. "Can't have you catching cold." He reached out and plucked Sabrina's dark wide-brimmed hat from a peg and placed it neatly on her head. "This'll keep your head warm."

"Thanks." She pushed the hat firmly in place.

"Anytime, Sam." His face was unperturbed as he pulled his own sheepskin jacket over his flannel shirt and jeans.

On the way to the stables, Samantha increased her pace to a trot to keep up with Jake's long, careless stride. Despite herself, she admired the confident, loose-limbed grace of his movement. He took his time, she noted, deciding he probably did nothing quickly, and more than likely still finished ahead of everyone else.

The dapple gray had been saddled and led outside by a smiling ranch hand.

"Howdy, ma'am. Dan said to have Spook ready for you."

"Thanks." She returned his friendly smile and patted the gelding's neck. "But I could have done it. I don't like to give you extra work."

"No trouble, ma'am. Dan said you weren't to do a lick of work today. You just go and have yourself a good time, and I'll rub old Spook down when you get back."

Samantha vaulted easily onto the horse's back, happy to feel a mount beneath her again. Riding was an old pleasure, to be enjoyed only when finances allowed.

"Now, you take good care of Miss Evans, Jake," the cowboy admonished with a conspirator's wink Samantha failed to catch. "Dan sets great store by this little lady."

Little again, Samantha thought.

"Don't you worry about Miss Evans, Lon." Jake mounted his stallion with a fluid motion. Again Samantha noticed that he wasted no time on superfluous movement. "I intend to keep a close eye on her."

Samantha acknowledged Jake's statement with a wrinkled nose, then, following the direction his hand indicated, set off in a brisk canter.

As the neat cluster of ranch buildings was left behind, her irritation vanished. The rushing air was exciting, filling her lungs and whipping roses into her cheeks. She had almost forgotten the sense of liberation riding gave her. It was the same sensation that she had experienced many times when flying from top to bottom or springing high in a double twist.

They rode in silence for a quarter of an hour. Jake allowed her to fill her being with the thrill of movement and the beauty of the countryside. Wild peaks jutted arrogantly into the sky. The rolling plains below were yellow-green with winter. They rode by Herefords, white-faced and sleek, who noted their passing with a lazy turn of the head before resuming their grazing.

A shape darted across an open field, and Samantha slowed her horse to a walk and pointed. "What's that?"

"Antelope," Jake answered, narrowing his eyes against the sun.

"Oh!" She halted her mount and watched the animal's graceful, bounding progress until it streaked over a hill and out of her view. "It must be marvelous to run like that, graceful and free." She turned her unguarded face to the man beside her and found him regarding her intently. His eyes held an expression she did not understand. A strange tingling raced along her spine, like warm fingers on cold skin. The tingling increased, the sensation spreading to settle somewhere in her stomach. Suddenly, his expression changed. The shadows of his face shifted as his lips moved into a smile.

"Someday you will be caught, little antelope."

She blinked at him, totally disoriented, trying to remember what they had been talking about. His grin increased. He pointed to a large, bare-limbed tree a quarter of a mile away.

"Race you." There was challenge under the lazy dare.

Her eyes brightened with excitement. "Fine

chance I'd have against a horse like that. What handicap do I get?"

Jake pushed his hat back as if to view her more completely. "From the look of you, I'd say you've got a good fifty-pound advantage. That should balance the odds some."

"No head start?"

"No, ma'am."

She pouted for a moment, then grinned. "All right, Jake Tanner, I'll give you a run for your money."

"Whenever you say, Sam." He pulled the brim of his hat low over his forehead.

"Now!"

She met the gelding's sides with her heels and spurted forward in a gallop. The quiet morning air vibrated with the thunder of hooves. Samantha, her hair flowing behind her, gave herself over to the thrill of the race. She reached the finish just ahead of her competitor and reined in, filling the morning with dusty, breathless laughter.

"Oh, that was wonderful, absolutely wonderful."

"Any time you want to give up teaching, Sam, you can work for me. I can use a hand who rides like you."

"I'll keep that in mind, even though I know you let me beat you."

"Now what makes you think that?" He leaned his arm on the horn of his saddle and watched her thoughtfully.

"I'm not stupid." Her grin was good-natured and friendly. "I couldn't beat that Arabian in a million years. You, maybe," she added with a touch of arrogance, "but not that horse."

"Pretty sharp, aren't you?" he returned, answering her grin.

"As a tack," she agreed. "And," she continued, brushing her hair from her shoulders, "I am not a weak female who needs to be placated. With my background, I know how to compete, I know how to lose, and —" she grinned and lifted her brows "— I know how to win."

"Point taken." He tilted his head as if to view her from a different angle. "From now on, Sam, we play head-to-head." He smiled, and she was no longer sure they were talking about the same thing. "I know how to win, too," he added slowly. They continued at a leisurely pace for a time, crossing a narrow branch of the Medicine Bow River. They paused there for the horses to quench their thirst in the icy water that forced its way over shining rocks with hisses and whispers. At Samantha's request, Jake began to identify the surrounding mountains.

Pointing to the long fingers of peaks at the south, the Laramie Range, he told her they extended from eastern Colorado. The middle section was the Medicine Bow Range, and the Sierra Madre loomed to the west. The vast ranges were separated by broad tongues of the

Wyoming Basin. Silver-blue, they gleamed in the sunlight, lacings of snow trembling from their summits.

She had reined in without being aware of her action. "I can never look at them long enough. I suppose you're used to them."

"No." There was no laughter or mockery in his tone. "You never get used to them."

She smiled a bit uncertainly, not at all sure she could deal with this side of him.

"Are there bears up there?" she asked.

He glanced up at the mountains, smiled, then looked back at her. "Black bear and grizzly," he informed her. "Elk, coyotes, mountain lions . . ."

"Mountain lions?" she repeated, a little nervously.

"You're not likely to run into one down here," he returned with an indulgent smile.

She ignored the mockery in his voice and looked around her, again awed by the miles of open space. "I wonder if this looked the same a century ago."

"Some of it. Those don't change much." He indicated the Rockies with an inclination of his head. "The Indians are gone," he continued, as if thinking aloud. "There were Arapaho, Sioux, Cheyenne, Crow, Shoshone, all roaming free over the state before the first white man set foot here. Then trappers came, trading with Indians, dressing like them, living like them, and the beaver was nearly driven into extinction." He

46

turned back to her, as if suddenly remembering she was there. "You're the teacher." His smile appeared. "You should be telling me."

Samantha shook her head in mock despair. "My knowledge of Wyoming's history is limited to late-night westerns." They were walking their horses slowly, side by side. She had completely forgotten her aversion to the man beside her. "It's impossible to believe the killing and cruelty that must have gone on here. It's so serene, and so vast. It seems there would have been room enough for everyone."

This time it was Jake who shook his head. "In 1841 more than a hundred and fifty thousand people crossed the South Pass going west, and a few years later, fifty thousand more came through on their way to California looking for gold. This was Indian land, had been Indian land for generations. Game disappeared, and when people get hungry, they fight. Treaties were signed, promises made by both sides, broken by both sides." He shrugged.

"In the 1860s, they tried to open the Bozeman Pass from Fort Laramie to Montana, and open war broke out. The trail ran through the Sioux hunting ground. The fighting was of the worst kind, massacres, indiscriminate killing of women and children, butcheries by both white and Indian. More treaties were signed, more misunderstandings, more killing, until the whites outnumbered the Indians, drove them away or put them on reservations."

"It doesn't seem fair," Samantha whispered, feeling a wave of sadness wash over her.

"No, it doesn't." He heard the wistful note in her voice and turned to regard her. "Life isn't always fair, though, is it, Samantha?"

"I suppose not." She sighed. "You seem to know quite a bit about what happened here. You must have had a good history teacher."

"I did." He held her curious look with a teasing half-smile on his lips. "My great-grandmother lived to be ninety-eight. She was Sioux."

Samantha lifted her brows in surprised interest. "Oh, I'd love to have met her. The things she must have seen, the changes in nearly a century of living."

"She was quite a woman." His smile faded a moment. "She taught me a lot. Among other things, she told me that the land goes on no matter who walks on it, that life moves on whether you fight against it or flow with it, that when you want something, you go after it until it's yours."

Suddenly, she felt he was leading her out of her depth, reaching for something she was not sure she possessed. She turned from the directness of his eyes to search the land.

"I'd like to have seen all this before there were any fences, before there was any fighting."

Jake pointed skyward. Glancing up, Samantha watched the graceful flight of an eagle. For a timeless moment, he soared overhead, the undisputed sovereign of the skies. They moved off again, in companionable silence. "I hope you're getting some fun out of this trip, some compensation for taking care of your sister," Jake said at last.

"I don't need any compensation for taking care of Bree, she's my sister, my . . ."

"Responsibility?"

"Well . . . yes. I've always looked out for Bree, she's more delicate, more . . . dependent than I am." She shrugged and felt uncomfortable without knowing why. "Dad always joked that I took my share of strength and half of Bree's while we were still in the womb. She needs me," she added, feeling compelled to defend what she had always taken for granted.

"She has Dan," Jake reminded her. "And she's a grown woman now — just as you are. Did it ever occur to you that you have your own life to lead now that Sabrina has a husband to care for her?"

"I'm not trying to take over for Dan," she said quickly. "Perhaps you can figure out how he could see to her needs and tend to the house and the ranch all at the same time, but I can't." She glared at him, half in anger, half in exasperation. "What do you expect me to do? Sit up in Philadelphia teaching kids to jump on a tramp while my sister needs help?"

"No, Samantha." He met her eyes with a quiet patience that was more disturbing than angry words and shouts. "What you're doing is very kind and unselfish."

49

"There's nothing kind or unselfish about it," she interrupted, shrugging the words away. "We're sisters. More than that, we're twins. We shared life from its beginning. You can't understand the kind of bond that creates. I'd give up a hundred jobs to help Bree if she needed me."

"No one's condemning your loyalty, Samantha. It's an admirable trait." He gave her a long, level look. "Just a word of advice. Don't become so involved that you forget who Samantha Evans is, and that she just might have the right to her own woman's life."

Samantha drew herself up to her full height in the saddle. "I hardly need your advice on how to run my life. I've been managing nicely for some time now."

His face creased in a lazy smile. "Yes, ma'am, I'm sure you have."

Chapter 4

Samantha had been riding the dapple gray in stubborn silence for nearly thirty minutes when she noticed more cattle. Her guide seemed unperturbed by her silence and slowed his Arabian's gait to the gelding's meandering walk. She would never have admitted to the man at her side that his words had disturbed her peace of mind.

What business was it of his how she chose to run her life? What gave Jake Tanner the right to question her relationship with Sabrina? No one asked him for his advice. And why in heaven's name should anything he said matter in the first place?

They were approaching a large ranch house. A redwood porch skirted the building's front, graced by evergreen shrubs. A gray wisp of smoke rose in a welcoming spire from the chimney. Ranch buildings sat neat and unobtrusive in the background.

"Welcome to the Double T, ma'am."

Jake drew her eyes with the uncharacteristic

51

formality in his tone. She turned to see him smile and touch the brim of his well-worn Stetson.

"Thank you, Mr. Tanner. I can honestly say your ranch is spectacular. But what, may I ask, are we doing here?"

"Well, now . . ." Jake shifted in the saddle to face her directly. "I don't know about you, but nearly three hours in the saddle gives me a powerful appetite. I figured here we might do a bit better than beef jerky."

"Three hours?" Samantha repeated, and pushed Sabrina's hat from her head so it lay against her back. "Has it really been that long?"

The angles of his face moved slowly with his grin, and she found herself once more intrigued by the process. "I'll take that to mean you were so delighted with my company, time stood still."

She answered with a toss of her head. "I hate to tread on your ego, Jake, but the credit goes to Wyoming."

"Close enough for now." Reaching over, he plopped the brimmed hat back in place on Samantha's head and urged his mount into a canter.

Samantha stared after him in exasperation, watching the confidence with which he rode the Arabian. They moved like one form rather than horse and man. Scowling, she pressed her heels to the gelding's side and raced forward to join him.

As she reached his side, he skirted the ranch

house and rode toward the buildings in the rear, following the left fork on a long, hard-packed road. A large, sleepy-eyed Saint Bernard rose from his siesta and romped forward to greet them. A deep, hoarse bark emitted from his throat. Jake halted in front of the stables. He slid off the Arabian's back, running his hand through the dog's thick fur as he hit the ground.

"Wolfgang's harmless." He acknowledged the loving, wet kisses with another brief caress and moved to the gelding's side. "He's just a puppy."

"A puppy," Samantha repeated. "You don't see many hundred-and-fifty-pound puppies." Tilting her head, she gave the overgrown baby a thorough examination before she brought her leg over the saddle to dismount.

Jake gripped her waist as she made her descent, holding her off the ground a moment as if she were weightless. As her boots touched earth, she was turned around and drawn against a hard chest. She tilted her head to inform him that his assistance was unnecessary, but saw only a brief blur of his face before his lips captured hers.

Her mind whirled with the touch and scent of him. She felt as though she were falling into a deep well and her heart began to beat a mad tempo against her ribs. She clutched at his jacket in defense. Perhaps the kiss was brief. It could have lasted no more than a portion of a minute, but it felt like forever. She knew his mouth was warm and sure on hers while decades flew into centuries.

The strange sensations of timelessness and loss of control frightened her. She stiffened and began to struggle against his grasp. He released her immediately, staring down at her clouded blue eyes with a satisfied smile. The smile transformed terror into fury.

"How dare you?"

"Just testing, ma'am." His answer was complacent, as though the kiss had been no more than that, a traditional touching of lips.

"Testing?" she repeated, running an agitated hand through her hair. "Testing what?"

"I've always wanted to kiss a teacher." Grinning, he gave her a friendly pat on the cheek. "I think there're some holes in your education."

"I'll show you holes, you conceited, high-handed —" her mind searched for something appropriately derogatory and settled on a generality "— *man*. If I didn't consider that kiss so insignificant, you'd be lying on your back checking out the sky."

He surveyed her as she trembled with a mixture of fury and wounded pride. He rubbed his chin thoughtfully. "You know, Sam, I almost believe you could do it."

"You can bank on it," she confirmed with an arrogant toss of her head. "And the next time you . . ." Feeling her arm sharply pulled, she glanced down to see the sleeve of her jacket captured in the awesome jaws of the Saint Bernard.

"What'd you do, teach him to eat unwilling females?"

"He just wants to make your acquaintance," Jake laughed, as he led the horses to the stable to turn them over to one of his men.

Samantha was not normally timid, and her pride refused to allow her to call Jake to untangle her from the teeth of his puppy. She swallowed and spoke to her canine captor.

"Hello . . . Wolfgang, wasn't it?" she muttered. "I'm Sam. You, ah, wouldn't consider letting go of my jacket, would you?" The dog continued to stare with droopy, innocent eyes. "Well, that's all right," she said, trying out magnanimity. "It's just an old one, anyway. I'm very fond of dogs, you know." Tentatively, she brought her free hand up to touch the fur on his huge head. "Well, actually, I have a cat," she admitted in apology, "but I have absolutely no prejudices."

Though his expression did not alter, she decided it was prudent to give him time for consideration. Her patience was rewarded when he released her sleeve and bathed her hand with his enormous tongue.

"Well, I see you two have made friends," Jake drawled, coming up behind her.

"No thanks to you," she said. "He might have eaten me alive."

"Not you, Sam," Jake disagreed, taking her hand and striding toward the house. "Too tough for Wolfgang's taste."

Jake led her to the back entrance through a paneled, tiled-floor mudroom and into the kitchen. A large square room, it was bright and cheery with tangerine curtains framing the wide windows. The pleasant-looking woman who stood by the sink smiled at Samantha. "Jake, you scoundrel, have you had this poor little lady out in the cold all this time?" Samantha met the warm brown eyes with a returning smile.

Jake grinned, unabashed. "Samantha Evans, meet Annie Holloway, my cook, housekeeper and best girl."

"Don't you try soft soaping me, you young devil." She brushed off his words with indulgent affection, but pleased color rose to her pudgy cheeks. "Thinks he can get around me with sweet talk. Pleased to meet you, Miss Evans." Samantha found her hand enclosed in a firm grip.

"Hello, Miss Holloway, I hope I'm not putting you out."

"Putting me out?" Annie let out a rich, full laugh, her ample bust heaving with the sound. "Isn't she the sweet one? Don't you be silly, now, and you just call me Annie like everyone else."

"Thank you, Annie." Samantha's smile warmed. "Everyone calls me Sam."

"Now that's a pretty thing," Annie commented, peering candidly into Samantha's face. "Yes, sir, a right pretty thing. You two run along," she commanded with an attempt at sternness. "Out of my kitchen. Lunch will be along, and I'll bring you in some tea to warm you up. Not you," she said with a scowl as Jake grimaced. "For the little lady. You don't need any warming up."

"Annie runs things," Jake explained as he led Samantha down a wide hall into the living room.

"I can see she does, even when she's securely wrapped around your little finger."

For a moment, his smile was so boyish and full of mischief, she nearly gave in to the urge to brush the curls from his forehead.

The paneling in the living room was light. The expanse of wood was broken by a large stone fireplace and wide windows framed with cinnamon-colored sheers. The dark gleaming furniture had been upholstered in gold, burnt sienna and rich browns. There was a comfortable hodgepodge of Hepplewhites and Chippendales with piecrust tilt-top tables and Pembrokes, ladder-back chairs and candlestands. In the center of the hardwood floor lay a wide rug of Indian design, so obviously old and handworked, that Samantha wondered if it had been his great-grandmother's fingers that had hooked it perhaps nearly a century ago. The room reflected a quiet, understated wealth, a wealth she somehow did not associate with the rangy, brash cowboy side of Jake.

A Charles Russell painting caught her eye. She turned to study it, attempting to sort out her new impressions of this complex man. Turning back, she found him watching her reaction with unconcealed amusement.

"I have a feeling you were expecting bearskins and oilcloth."

Samantha focused her attention on the inviting fire. "I never know what to expect from you," she muttered.

"No?" He dropped his lanky form into a wing-backed chair and pulled out a long, thin cigar. "I thought you were pretty bright."

Samantha seated herself in the chair across from him, keeping the warmth and hiss of the fire between them. "This is a lovely room, very appealing and very warm."

"I'm glad you like it." If he noticed her blatant change of subject, he gave no sign. Lighting his cigar, he stretched out his legs and looked totally relaxed and content.

"I have a weakness for antiques," she continued, deciding the topic was safe and impersonal.

He smiled, the smoke curling lazily above his head. "There's a piece in one of the bedrooms you might like to see. A blanket chest in walnut that was brought over from the East in the 1860s."

"I'd like that very much." She returned his smile and settled back as Annie wheeled a small tea cart into the room.

"I brought you coffee," she said to Jake, and passed him a cup. "I know you won't take tea unless you douse it with bourbon. Something not quite decent about doing that to a good cup of tea."

"Tea is an old ladies' drink," he stated, ignoring her rapidly clucking tongue.

"How do you think Sabrina looks?" Samantha asked him when Annie had bustled back to the kitchen.

"I think you worry too much about her."

She bristled instinctively before replying. "Perhaps you're right," she surprised herself by admitting. "Our mother always said Bree and I were mirror images, meaning, I discovered after a while, opposites."

"Right down to Sabrina being right-handed, and you being left."

"Why, yes." She looked at him in faint surprise. "You don't miss much, do you?" He merely shook his head and gave her an enigmatic smile. "Well," she plunged on, not sure she liked his expression, a bit like a cat who already had the mouse between his paws. "I suppose the summary of my discrepancies was that I could never keep the hem in my white organdy party dress. You'd have to know my mother to understand that. She would have Bree and me all decked out in these frilly white organdy dresses and send us off to a party. Bree would come back spotless, pure and angelic. I'd come back with dirt on my frills, bloody knees and a trailing hem."

During her story, Jake's smile had widened.

The coffee in his cup cooled, unattended as he watched her. "There're doers and there're watchers, Samantha. I imagine you had fun scraping up your knees."

As ridiculous as it seemed, she felt she'd just been complimented, and was both pleased and faintly embarrassed.

"I suppose you're a doer, too." She dropped her eyes. "You couldn't run a ranch like this and not be. Cattle ranching sounds romantic, but I imagine it's long hours, hot summers and cold winters. I don't suppose it's really all that different from the way it used to be a hundred years ago."

"The range isn't open anymore," he corrected. "You don't find cowboys going off to Texas to punch cattle with a ten-dollar horse and a forty-dollar saddle." He shrugged and set his empty cup on the table beside him. "But some change slow, and I'm one who likes to take my time."

She was frowning into his smile when Annie announced lunch. It was not until they were settled in the dining room that she spoke directly to him again, pressing him for more details on how the ranch was run.

He explained how roundups, which had once been accomplished on the vast open range with only men and horses, were now aided by fences and technology. But it was still men and ponies who moved the cattle into corrals. Over a few states there were still strongholds of riders and ropers, men who cultivated the old technique and blended it with the new. On the Double T, Jake employed the best of both.

"If roundups aren't what they once were, they still accomplish the same end. Getting the cattle together and branding them."

"Branding?" Samantha interrupted, and shuddered.

"Your Philadelphia's showing, Sam." He grinned. "Take my word for it, branding is a good deal more unpleasant for the branders than the brandees."

She decided to ignore his comments and changed the subject abruptly. "Bree told me your ranch borders Dan's. This place must be huge for it to have taken us three hours to get here."

Jake's deep, rich laughter filled the room, and she decided unwillingly that she liked the sound very much. "It's a pretty big spread, Sam, but if you take the straight road north for the Lazy L, you can be here in twenty minutes on horseback. I took you on a big circle today," he explained. "Just a small taste of our part of the Laramie Basin."

They lingered over coffee, relaxed in each other's company.

"We'd better get started back," Jake said after a while. He rose and extended his hand. Her own slipped without hesitation into it as he pulled her to her feet. When she looked up at him, her smile was warm and spontaneous.

"Annie was right, that's a pretty thing." He lifted his hand and traced his fingers over the curve of her mouth. She started. "Now don't go skittish on me, Sam, I'm not going to use spurs and a whip."

His mouth lowered, gentle and persuasive. One hand held hers while the other circled the back of her neck to soothe with coaxing fingers. She had only to sway forward to feel his body against hers, had only to lift her hand to bring his mouth firmer and warmer on hers. Before the choice could be made, he drew her away and the decision was taken out of her hands.

"Sam." He shook his head as if exasperated and lightly amused. "You're enough to try a man's patience."

With this, he pulled her through to the kitchen.

"Well, so you're off again." Annie wiped one hand on her apron and wagged the other at Jake. "And don't be keeping her out in that cold too long."

"No, ma'am," Jake returned with suspicious respect.

"Thank you, Annie," Samantha broke in. "Lunch was wonderful."

"Well, now, that's fine, then." She gave Samantha a friendly pat on the cheek. "You just come back real soon, and you say hi to Sabrina for me, and that young rascal Dan, too. As soon as she's fit again, I'll be coming by to see her. Oh, Jake, I clean forgot." Annie turned to him and sighed at her absentmindedness. "Lesley Marshall called earlier, something about dinner tonight. I told her you'd give her a call, then it went straight out of my mind."

"No problem," Jake said easily. "I'll get back to her later. Ready, Sam?"

"Yes, I'm ready." She kept her smile in place, though a large black cloud seemed to have suddenly smothered the sunshine.

Lesley Marshall, she mused, automatically going through the motions of securing her hat and coat. That was the woman Bree had predicted would marry Jake when he decided to settle down. Why should it matter to me? She straightened her spine and accompanied Jake to the waiting horses. I have absolutely no interest in Jake Tanner's affairs.

He's probably had dozens of girlfriends. Well, it's no concern of mine. Vaulting into the saddle, she followed as he set off down the hard-packed road.

They spoke little on the return journey. Samantha pretended an engrossment with the scenery that she was far from feeling. Unhappily, she realized Wyoming's magic was not quite enough to lift her flagging spirits. Snow-capped peaks glistened just as brightly in the late afternoon sun, and the land still spread and beckoned, but as she surveyed them now she felt strangely depressed.

It had been an unusual day, she concluded. Jake had annoyed her, charmed her, angered her and delighted her, all in a handful of hours. His kiss had aroused excitement and a deeper feeling she could not explain.

The knowledge that he was dining with another woman that evening depressed her beyond belief. She stole a sidelong look at his lean, tanned features.

He was undeniably attractive, she admitted, pulling her eyes away from him before he could sense her study. There was a powerful aura of virility about him, which alternately intrigued her and made her wary. Perhaps it would be wise to avoid his company. He confused her, and Samantha liked to know precisely where she stood with a man. She wanted to call the shots, and she realized that this man would never allow anyone to call the shots but himself.

She would keep her distance from now on. Let him spread his charm over this Lesley Marshall, or any of the other women who were undoubtedly thirsting for his attention. Samantha Evans could get along very easily without him. As the Lazy L grew closer, she resolved to be polite and casually friendly to her escort. After all, she reflected, there was no reason to be rude. He was perfectly free to dine with whomever he chose; his life was most assuredly his own. Besides, she added to herself, if she had anything to say about it, they would be seeing very little of each other in the future.

When they reached the ranch, she dismounted, handing Spook's reins to a waiting cowboy. "I had a wonderful time, Jake." Samantha's smile was faultless in its social politeness as he walked her toward the ranch house, leading his stallion behind him. "I appreciate your time and hospitality."

Jake's mouth lifted at one corner. "It was my pleasure, ma'am."

If there was a mockery in his tone, Samantha chose to ignore it. Reaching the back door, she turned to smile at him again as he stood, tall and lean, beside the gleaming chestnut.

"Would you like some coffee before you go?" she invited, determined to be polite.

"No, thanks, Sam." He continued to watch her, his eyes shaded by the brim of his hat. "I'd best be getting along."

"Well." She breathed a small sigh of relief when her hand touched the doorknob and safety was in easy reach. "Thanks again."

"Sure." He nodded briefly and turned to his horse, paused and turned back to look at her with a penetrating intensity that turned her legs to water. When he spoke, it was soft and final. "I mean to have you, you know."

Several moments of silence passed before she could summon up an answer.

"D-Do you?" Her voice was a shaky whisper, unlike the coolly flippant tone she would have wished for.

"Yes, ma'am." He vaulted onto the chestnut's back and pushed the Stetson back on his head so that she had a disturbingly clear view of his eyes. "I do," he confirmed, turning his mount and galloping away.

Chapter 5

Often over the next few days, Samantha told herself that her reaction to Jake's kiss had been merely a passing physical attraction. She was a normal woman, wasn't she? So why feel guilty about it?

Jake Tanner *was* a very attractive man. *Too attractive,* she added to herself. And he knew too much about charming women. The fact that Jake was abrasive, smug and irritating had nothing to do with the way she had acted. It had just been a passing fancy. *And would certainly not occur again.*

Finally Sabrina was allowed up from the confinement of her bed. Samantha decided it was safe to leave her sister for a few hours. With a light heart, she saddled Spook and set off from the ranch at a brisk canter. For a while she enjoyed the feeling of Spook's hooves pounding the hard road. The sky hung low above her, and heavy, leaden gray clouds draped the distant mountains in mysterious gloom. There was a stillness, a waiting in the air, unnoticed by Samantha in her eagerness to escape the close confines of the house.

She rode swiftly past the bored, white-faced cattle and the stretches of barbed wire, eager to explore new territory, tasting the joy of motion and freedom. The mountains, grim sentinels above her, stood stone-gray under the unbroken sky. Remembering Dan's instructions, Samantha took care to mark her route, choosing a clump of rocks, a cottonwood tree with a broken limb, and a gnarled stump as landmarks for her return trip.

She led her mount to a crest of a hill, watching as a jackrabbit, startled by her intrusion, darted across the road and out of sight.

Nearly an hour passed before the first flakes began to drift lazily from sky to earth. She stopped and watched their progress in fascination. The snow fell slowly. Lifting her face, she let it caress her cheeks and closed lids. The air was moist, coming to life around her, and she stirred herself out of her dream.

"Well, Spook, this is my first Wyoming snow. I'd like to stay here all day and watch it fall, but duty calls. We'd better head back." Patting the horse's neck, she turned back toward the ranch.

They rode slowly. Samantha was enchanted with the fairyland that was forming around her. Cottonwoods and aspens were draped in white, their branches a stark contrast to the brilliant etchings of snow. The ground was cloaked quickly. Though the beauty was breathtaking, Samantha began to feel uncomfortably alone.

She took Spook into a canter. The sound of his hooves was soft and muffled. The quiet surrounding her was unearthly, almost as though the world had ceased to breathe. She shivered, suddenly cold in the warm confines of her jacket. To her annoyance, she saw that in her preoccupation with the landscape she had taken a wrong turn, and she began to backtrack, berating herself for carelessness.

The snow increased, plunging down from a sky she could no longer see. She cursed herself for having come so far, fighting down a sudden surge of panic. "Don't be silly, Sam," she spoke aloud, wanting the reassurance of her own voice. "A little snow won't hurt you."

The cold became more intense, piercing the layers of her skin. Samantha tried to concentrate on steaming coffee and a blazing fire as she looked around for a familiar landmark. Nothing was the same as it had been. She clamped her lips tight to still the chattering of her teeth, telling herself that it was impossible that she could be lost. But it was a lie. The trees and hills around her were strangers blanketed in white.

The snow fell thickly, a blinding white wall blocking her vision. A wind had sprung up, breaking the silence with its moans and tossing snow, hard and bitter, into her face. She was forced to slow the gelding to a walk, afraid of tangling with the sharp teeth of barbed wire she was unable to see. Her teeth savaged her lips in an effort to control a growing terror.

It's so cold, she thought as she began to shiver convulsively, so unbelievably cold.

The snow had soaked through the wool of her slacks and slipped mercilessly down the neck of her coat. She hunched her shoulders against the driving wind. Snow was everywhere, blocking her in and seeping into her clothing.

She let the reins hang limp, praying that the horse's instinct would guide him back to the warm shelter of his stables. They trudged on, the vortex of white that had begun so innocently now whirling around her. Time and direction had lost all meaning, and though she tried calling out, her voice was soundless against the fierce breath of the wind.

Now she felt the cold. Her body was numbed into submission. Her mind was following suit. The swirling snow was hypnotic, and a growing lethargy was creeping over her. In a small part of her mind, she knew her survival depended on remaining alert.

Horse and rider plodded on. There was no time, no world beyond the unbroken curtain of white. Samantha felt her eyelids growing heavy, but she willed them open with all her strength. The snow piled onto her back, weighing her down until she slumped onto the gelding's mane and clung to him. Staring down at the gelding's front hoof, she began to count each drudging step that Spook took as he continued his slow progress through the blinding storm.

Samantha's concentration on the horse's halting steps began to fade.

If I close my eyes, she thought dimly, I won't see all that white and I can sleep. Oh, how I want to sleep. . . .

The snow was talking, she mused deliriously. Well, why not? It's alive. Why should it sound like Jake? Helplessly, she began to giggle. Well, why shouldn't it? *They both play to win.*

"Samantha!" The snow was shouting at her. "Open your eyes. Stop that insane laughing and open your eyes!"

Wearily, she forced herself to obey the command. Dimly she saw the blur of Jake's features through the flurries of snow. "You would be the last thing I see before I die." With a moan, she closed her eyes again and sought the silence.

"Tell Dan we've found her," Jake shouted against the howl of the wind. "I'm taking her back to the Double T."

The darkness was comforting. Samantha gave herself over to it, feeling herself falling slowly into a hole with no bottom. She burrowed deeper into it. Her consciousness swam to the surface.

Bemused, she looked around a dimly lit room. The snow that pooled around her was not snow at all, but a bed with a thick, warm quilt. She allowed her heavy lids to close again.

"Oh, no, you don't." The lids opened fractionally, and Samantha saw Jake standing in the open doorway.

"Hello."

His mouth thinned as he advanced to the bed to tower over her. It seeped through the misty reaches of her brain that he was angry. She stared at him with lazy fascination.

"What in heaven's name were you doing out in such a storm? I've seen some dumb stunts, but taking a joyride in the middle of a blizzard tops them all."

She wanted to ask him to stop shouting at her, but lacked the energy. "Where am I?" was all she could find to say.

Sitting on the edge of the bed, he drew her head from the pillow, then held a cup to her lips. "Here, drink this first, then we'll talk."

The brandy was warm and strong, and she sputtered and gasped as he poured it down her throat. Its power spread through her, pushing back the mists of unconsciousness.

"Now, to answer your question, you're at the Double T." Jake set the empty cup aside, and laid her head back on the mound of pillows.

"Oh."

"Is that all you can say?" He was shouting again. He took her shoulders as if to shake her. "Just 'Oh'? What in heaven's name were you doing out there?"

"It seems so long ago." She frowned in concentration, closing her eyes with the effort. "It wasn't snowing when I left," she said in weak defense.

"*Wasn't snowing?*" Jake repeated, incredulous. "Samantha, didn't you see the sky? Where are your brains?"

"There's no excuse for insults," she retorted with a small flash of spirit.

"No excuse for insults? Are you stark raving mad? Do you realize what nearly happened to you?" His hands retreated to his pockets, as though he could barely prevent them from throttling her. "Out here in the middle of a blizzard, half-frozen and helplessly lost! It was a miracle we found you. A little longer, and you'd be lying somewhere buried in it, and no one would have found what was left until spring. Dan was half out of his mind when he got through to me and told me you'd gone out in this."

"Bree?"

"Knew nothing." He whirled to face her again. "She was taking a nap. It never occurred to her that you had gone out with a storm brewing." He laughed harshly.

The memory of the snow and the terror washed over her, and she began to shake. "I'm sorry," she managed through the tears that threatened to flow. With a brief oath, Jake ran a hand through his hair. He closed the distance between them and gathered her in his arms. "Samantha," he murmured against her hair. "What hell you put us all through."

"I'm sorry," she repeated, and she began to sob in earnest. "I was so scared, so cold."

He rocked and murmured words she could not understand, his lips brushing through her hair and over her damp cheeks until they met hers. The kiss mingled with the salt of her tears. "I've gotten your shirt all wet," she murmured after a while.

He let out a deep breath. She saw his smile begin to spread before he rested his brow against hers. "That is without doubt the worst calamity of the day."

"It's dark," she said with sudden realization. "How long . . . ?"

"Too long. What you need now is rest."

"Spook?" she began as he lay her down on the pillows.

"Is sleeping off his adventure in the stables. He looks a lot better than you, I might add."

"I want to thank you for everything." Samantha reached for his hand. In that instant, she discovered there was nothing covering her save sheets and blankets. "M-My clothes," she stammered, drawing the quilt higher in a purely feminine gesture that caused Jake's mouth to twitch.

"Soaked through, Sam." Rising, he stood, rocking gently on his heels. "It was necessary to get you warm and dry."

"Did Annie?" she managed a smile at the thought of the matronly presence of Jake's housekeeper. "I seem to have put everyone to a lot of trouble. Will you thank her for me?"

"Well, Sam, I'd like to oblige you, but Annie left yesterday for Colorado to spend a week with her nephew." Jake's grin broadened.

"Then who — ?" The question caught in her throat, and her eyes became round and impossibly dark. "Oh, no," she whispered, closing her eyes in humiliation.

"No need to be embarrassed, Sam, you have a beautiful body."

"Oh, no." With a moan, she squeezed her eyes tighter.

"Now, don't you fret." His tone took on the light insolence of the cowboy she'd met a month before in the cold March sunset. "When I took off your clothes and rubbed you down, it was strictly medical. I'd do as much for any stray." He patted her hand, and her eyes opened warily at his touch.

"Yes, of course." Moistening her lips, she attempted to see the practical side. "I, well . . . thank you."

" 'S all right, don't give it a thought." He moved toward the door, then paused and turned back. "Now, the next time I get your clothes off, my purposes'll be completely different."

He strolled casually from the room, leaving a speechless Samantha.

Chapter 6

Samantha looked around her. She remembered with a shock that she was in Jake's house — and, worse yet, *naked* in bed. She was debating the wisdom of wrapping the quilt around her and searching for more appropriate attire when footsteps sounded down the hall outside her room. She pulled the covers to her chin as Jake strode through the open door.

"So, you're awake. How do you feel?"

"Fine." Her respiratory system behaved erratically as he continued toward her and dropped onto the bed. "I'm just fine," she repeated, then added unnecessarily, "It's still snowing."

"So it is," he agreed without taking his eyes from her face. "Slowing down, though."

"Is it?" She forced herself to look out the window.

"The worst'll be over by midday." He reached up and pried one of her hands loose from the death grip on the blanket. "Calm down, Sam, I'm not going to ravish you, I'm going to check your pulse."

76

"I'm fine," she repeated again.

"Far from fine, Samantha," he corrected. His fingers brushed against her cheek, as if to test its substance. "The first thing is to get some food into you." Rising, he held out a large flannel robe that he had dropped at the foot of the bed. "You'd probably feel better if you had something on." His smile was gently mocking. "Can you manage to get into this by yourself?"

"Of course." Plucking it from him, she kept a cautious grip on the blankets. "I'm not an invalid."

"You best think like one. Put that on, then get back in bed. I'll bring you some breakfast."

"I don't . . ."

"Don't argue." The two words were swift and final. He was gone before she could say another word.

He had shut the door, however, and grateful for the concession, Samantha tossed back the covers and slipped her arm into the robe. When she stood, the room swayed and spun around her. She sank back onto the bed and slipped her other arm into its sleeve, pulling the robe around her before attempting to stand again. Her limbs felt heavy and weak, and she noted with puzzlement that her ankle was throbbing lightly. Gripping one poster of the bed until the room steadied, she rolled up the sleeves of the robe several times until her hands became visible, then moved to the bathroom to study herself in the mirror.

The sight of her own face caught at her breath. Her skin seemed nearly transparent, her eyes darker and larger in contrast. The breath of color that resulted when she pinched her cheeks faded instantly. She ran a hand through her hair falling on the shoulders of the dark green robe.

It must be his, she realized, looking down at the sleeves, which swallowed her arms, and the hem, which fell nearly to her ankles. A strange sensation flowed over her as she felt the material on her skin. Turning away from the mirror, she studied the bed.

"I'm not getting in there again," she muttered, and with a small gesture of defiance belted the robe more securely. "I can eat at the table like a normal person."

After a moment, her progress down the hall seemed more of a crawl than a walk. Her legs were heavy with a weakness which infuriated her. The stillness of the house vibrated around her, playing havoc with her nerves, and the need to hear the natural, everyday movements of another human being became increasingly important. She cursed the waves of giddiness that swam around in her head, forcing her to stop time after time to rest her hand against the wall.

"This is ridiculous."

"You're right."

The harsh agreement came from behind as Jake's hands gripped her shoulders.

"What are you doing out of bed?"

"I'm all right." She swayed against his chest.

He gripped her waist to support her, and she rested her hands on his arms.

"I'm just a bit wobbly, and I'm having some trouble with my ankle."

He let his gaze travel down to rest on her bare feet. "Probably turned it when you fell off the horse."

"I fell off Spook?" Her expression was incredulous.

"You were unconscious at the time. Now, get back in bed and stay there." Effortlessly, he swept her into his arms, and she laid her head against his shoulder.

"Jake, don't make me go back to bed. It's so quiet in there, and I don't feel like being alone now."

He bent and brushed lips that parted in confusion. "If you think you can sit in a chair without sliding on your face, you can come in the kitchen."

She nodded, sighed and closed her eyes. "I hate being so much trouble."

She felt him shift her in his arms before he began the journey down the hall. "I knew you were trouble the minute I set eyes on you."

"Don't tease, Jake, I'm trying to thank you."

"What for?"

She lifted a hand to his cheek, turning his face so that he would look at her. "For my life."

"Then take better care of it in the future," he suggested.

"Jake, please, I'm serious. I owe you . . ."

"Nothing, you owe me nothing." His voice had hardened with annoyance. "I don't want your gratitude." They had reached the kitchen, and he placed her in a chair at the table. "Which ankle did you hurt?" He crouched down by her feet.

"The left one. Jake, I — Ouch!"

"Sorry." He grinned up at her, then rested his hand with friendly ease on her knee. "It's not swollen."

"It still hurts," she said stubbornly.

"Keep off it, then," he advised with simple logic, and turned away to finish breakfast.

"You've got some bedside manners, Dr. Tanner," she observed sharply.

"Yes, ma'am, so I've been told." When he turned to face her, his smile was bland. "Tell me, Sam, does Sabrina have a mole on her left hip, too?"

Color flooded her face. "You . . . you . . ." she faltered, and clutched the robe tight at her throat.

"Around here, we call that locking the barn door after the cow's got loose. Have some coffee," he invited with sudden graciousness, pouring a cup and setting it on the table. "Start on this bacon," he ordered, sliding a plate in front of her. "That color didn't last long, you're pale as a ghost again. When did you eat last?"

"I . . . at breakfast yesterday, I guess."

"Toast and coffee, I imagine," he said disgustedly. "It's a wonder you can manage to sit up at all. Eat." He plucked a piece of bacon from the plate and held it out to her. "I'll have some eggs ready in a minute."

Obediently, she accepted the bacon and took a bite. "Are you going to have something?"

"In a minute," he answered absently, involved with breaking and beating eggs in a bowl.

With the first bite of bacon, Samantha realized she was ravenous. Through her preoccupation with food, she watched Jake cook with a deftness that amused and surprised her.

In a moment, he sat across from her, his plate piled high. She wondered how he could eat with such abandon and remain hard and lean.

She watched him under the cover of her lashes, and the thought came unbidden into her mind that never before had she shared the breakfast table with a man. The intimacy of their situation washed over her; the scent of bacon and coffee drifting through the air, the house quiet and empty around them, the soft flannel of his robe against her skin, the faint masculine scent of him clinging to it. It was as if they were lovers, she thought suddenly, as if they had shared the night, and now they were sharing the morning. Her face grew warm.

"I don't know what thought put roses back in those cheeks, Sam, but keep it up."

Her eyes lifted to his, and she had the uncomfortable feeling that he knew very well what

81

road her thoughts had taken. She dropped her eyes to her plate. "I should call Bree and let her know I'm all right."

"Phones are out," he said simply, and her eyes flew back to his.

"The phones are out?" she repeated.

No telephone, her mind said again. Without a telephone, they might as well be on an island a thousand miles from anyone. Their isolation was complete, and the snow was still falling as though it would never stop.

"With a storm like this, it's not surprising to lose the phones. Power's out, too. We're on generator. Don't worry about Sabrina, she knows you're with me." His words did nothing to erase her tension.

"When . . . when do you think I'll be able to get back?"

"Couple of days," he returned with an easy shrug, and sipped his coffee. "The roads'll have to be cleared after the storm lets up, and you're not in any shape to travel through a mess like that yet. In a day or two, you'll be more up to it."

"A couple of days?"

He leaned back comfortably in his chair, his voice smooth as a quiet river. "Of course, by then you'll be hopelessly compromised, not a scrap of your sterling reputation left. Alone with me for two or three days, without Annie to add a thread of decency to the situation." His eyes traveled down her slim figure. "Wearing my bathrobe, too." He shook his head. "Not too many years back, I'd have had to marry you."

"Thank goodness for progress," she retorted smartly.

"Oh, I don't know, Sam." His sigh was convincing. "I'm an old-fashioned sort of man."

"It's only a matter of circumstance that we're alone here in the first place." With great dignity, she folded her arms. "And I've hardly been compromised, as you so quaintly put it."

"No?" He watched her through lazily narrowed eyes. "So far, I've undressed you, tucked you in and fixed your breakfast. Who knows what that might lead to?"

His smile might have been lazy, but it was full of meaning. Suddenly Samantha found it difficult to swallow.

"Relax, Sam." His laugh was full of arrogant enjoyment. "I told you I mean to have you, but it's not in my plans to take on a pale child who barely has the strength to stand." He paused, lit one of his long, thin cigars and blew smoke at the ceiling. "When I make love to you, I want you to have your wits about you. I don't want you passing out in my arms."

The man's arrogance was amazing! "You conceited mule," she began. "How dare you sit there and tell me you're going to make love to me? You seem to think you're irresistible! Well, you have another thing coming —"

"I'm going to remind you of that one day, Sam," Jake said mildly as he crushed out his cigar. "Now, I think you better lie down again. You're not quite up to sparring with me yet."

"I do not have to lie down. And I certainly don't need you carting me around. I can manage." She stood up, then was forced to grasp the table as the room revolved around her.

"You don't look ready to turn cartwheels, teacher," Jake observed as he took her arm.

"I'm all right." Her hand, which she had lifted to push him away, lay weakly on his chest for support. He tilted her chin, and he was no longer smiling. "Samantha, sometimes you have to be strong enough to let someone else take care of things. You're going to have to hand over the reins to me for a couple of days. If you fight it, you're only going to make it harder on your-self."

With a sigh, she allowed her head to fall against his chest, not protesting as his arms encircled her. "Do I have to like it?"

"Not necessarily." He gave a short laugh and lifted her easily and carried her back to bed.

Her small spurt of energy deserted her. With an odd feeling of contentment, she settled down under the covers. She was asleep even before his lips had lightly touched her forehead in a fare-well kiss . . .

"I was beginning to think you'd sleep through the night."

She turned her head quickly. Jake was sitting across the room, the smoke of his cigar spiraling upward, the flickering lights from the fire shooting specks of gold into his eyes. Samantha brushed the tousled hair from her face and struggled into a sitting position.

"It's dark," she said. "What time is it?"

He glanced at the gold watch on his wrist and took a slow drag from his cigar. "It's a bit past six."

"Six? I've slept for hours. I feel as if I've slept for weeks."

"You needed it." Tossing the stub of his cigar into the mouth of the fire, Jake rose and moved toward her. His concerned eyes roamed over her sleep-flushed cheeks and heavy eyes. Gradually, his expression lightened, the angles of his face moving into a satisfied smile. "Your color's coming back." He took her wrist, and her eyes dropped from his to study the dancing flames of the fire. "Pulse's a bit jumpy." The smile reflected in his voice. "Strong though. Hungry?"

"I shouldn't be." She forced her eyes to meet his. "I've done nothing but lie around all day, but I'm starved."

He smiled again, lifting her without comment. She felt small and vulnerable in his arms, a sensation that was both pleasant and disturbing. She found it difficult to resist the impulse to rest her head against the strong curve of his shoulder. Instead, she concentrated on the sharp, clean lines of his profile.

"I'm sure I can walk. I really feel fine."

"I doubt it." She could feel his warm breath

on her face. "Besides, you seem to fit in my arms pretty well."

Finding no quick comeback to this comment, she took the journey to the kitchen in silence.

Leaning back in her chair, replete and content, Samantha sipped the cool white wine in her glass and gave Jake a nod of approval.

"You're going to make some woman a terrific husband. You're an outstanding cook."

"I think so." He nodded smugly. "My wife wouldn't have to be a gourmet cook," he added with casual consideration. "I'd demand other qualities."

"Adoration," Samantha suggested. "Obedience, unswerving loyalty, solicitude."

"That's all right for a start."

"Poor woman."

"Of course, I don't want her to be a doormat. Let's say I like a woman who knows how to think, one who doesn't pretend to be anything but who she is. Of course," he added, finishing off his wine, "I'm also partial to good looks."

"Well, so far it doesn't sound as though you're asking for much," Samantha giggled. "Just perfection."

"The woman I have in mind can handle it." He smiled broadly as he rose to pour coffee. Samantha stared at his back, feeling as though her heart had been dropped into a deep hole. *Lesley Marshall.* Her mind flashed the name like a neon sign in bright red letters.

Jake squelched her offer to do the dishes and swooped her from her chair and deposited her on the living room sofa.

"I feel useless," she muttered, helplessly cocooned by blankets and pillows. "I'm not made for lying around. I'm never sick." She gave Jake a sulky glare as if the entire matter was his fault. "I don't know how Bree coped with this sort of thing for a month."

"Could be you got her share of strength, and she got your share of patience," he considered, then shrugged. "Of course, I could be wrong." She heard his chuckle and the quiet click of his lighter as he lit a cigar.

Well, Samantha, she chided herself, you've really done it this time. Not only are you isolated with a man who constantly confuses you, but you can't even stand on your own feet. They say people learn about each other quickly when they live together, but I think it's going to take much more than one day to learn what this man is all about. *Living together,* she repeated, finding herself more amused than embarrassed. If Momma could see me now, we'd need a gallon of smelling salts.

Chapter 7

Dawn was breaking. Pink and gold streaks split the hazy blue of the sky, and light tumbled through to rest on Samantha's closed lids.

Morning? Sitting up with a start, she shook her head vigorously to dispel the last remnants of sleep. Pulling on the borrowed robe, she set her feet on the floor, took three deep breaths and stood. When both the room and her head remained stable, she let out a long sigh of relief. Her legs were weak, but they no longer felt as if they would melt from under her, and the stiffness in her ankle had disappeared.

Mobility, she thought with arrogant glee. I've never truly appreciated it until now. Coffee. One thought followed swiftly on the trail of the other, and she deserted the room with the intention of making fantasy fact. A door opened as she passed it, and with a cry of surprise, she fell against the opposite wall.

Jake stood in the doorway, rubbing a towel briskly through his damp hair, a terry-cloth robe tied loosely around his waist. "Morning, ma'am."

"You startled me." She swallowed, over-powered by the lean, bronzed maleness that the terry cloth did little to hide. He took a step toward her, and her breath caught instinctively. "I — I'm much better." She began to babble, unconsciously cowering against the smooth paneling. "I can actually walk a straight line."

Her voice died to a whisper as he stood directly in front of her. Her eyes were on a line with the tanned column of throat revealed by the open neck of the robe. His hand lifted her chin, and she trembled.

"Relax, Sam." His laughter sounded deep in his throat. "I just want to look you over. You must have the constitution of an elephant," he concluded with unflattering candor. "You look as though you've been on vacation instead of battling blizzards. One day's rest after nearly freezing to death. Most women would have been stretched out for a week."

"I'm not most women." She pushed his hand away from her face. "I'm not fragile and delicate, and I'm not going back to bed. I'm going to fix breakfast." She nudged him out of her path and started down the hall.

"Coffee's already on," he called after her.

Samantha had breakfast under way by the time Jake joined her. Clad in the less disturbing attire of corded jeans and flannel shirt, he watched her prepare the meal as he silently sipped at the coffee at the kitchen table.

"I'm getting used to having a pretty face across from me at breakfast," he commented when she sat down to join him.

"I'm sure I'm not the first," she commented with studied indifference. Nor, she added to herself, will I be the last.

"Nope," he agreed easily, "but there's something to be said for big blue eyes first thing in the morning."

"Blue eyes are common enough," she muttered, and lowered them to the contents of her plate. "Besides, this is hardly a long-term arrangement." He did not speak for a moment, and her fork moved restlessly among her eggs.

"We should have the road clear enough sometime tomorrow."

"Tomorrow?" she repeated. A hollow feeling spread through her stomach.

"There's a lot of snow out there, some of the drifts are small mountains. It's going to take a little time to move it."

"I see."

"Do you think you could manage on your own for a while today?"

"What? Oh, sure, I'll be fine."

"There's a lot I should see to. My foreman was in charge yesterday, but the men need all the help they can get." He was frowning. "Cattle need hay brought out to them. They haven't the sense to dig through to the grass. They'll just stand there and starve to death."

"I suppose the storm did a lot of damage."

"It's only minor from the reports I've gotten. We were hit worse a couple years ago."

"Reports?"

"One of my men came by yesterday afternoon to fill me in." Pouring more coffee in his cup, he reached for the cream. "You were asleep."

"Oh." Strange, she thought, there had been a ripple in their isolation and she had been totally unaware of it.

Lifting his cup, he studied her over the rim. "I don't like leaving you alone, especially with the phones out."

Her shoulders moved. "Don't worry about me, I'll be fine." Glancing up, she met his speculative gaze.

"I don't know how long I'll be gone."

"Jake, stop fussing. I feel fine."

He tilted his head to the side, his eyes still narrowed. "Stand up. I want to see how you feel for myself."

Before she realized his intent, his arms were around her, and his mouth was on hers. Her legs buckled.

His mouth was light, teasing, his teeth nibbling at the fullness of her bottom lip until she moaned from the exquisite agony. She gripped his shoulders as a dim light of control seeped into the darkness. Pulling away she shook her head in refusal.

"Now, Sam . . ." His voice was soft and persuasive, but the hands that descended to her hips were firm. "You wouldn't send a man out in the cold without something warm to remember, would you?"

Insistently, he brought her closer, molding her hips, exploring the soft roundness until she was pressed against him with exciting intimacy. His mouth closed over her protest, his tongue moving with slow devastation to tease hers until she felt the room spinning as wildly as it had the day before. Slowly, his hands ascended, his thumbs circling the side of her breasts while his mouth and tongue destroyed all resistance. She was straining against him, moving against him, reason forgotten. Her body heated urgently at his touch. Her sigh was a moan as his mouth descended to her throat. His lips tasted, lingered, traveled to new territories, the tip of his tongue moist and warm against her skin, erotic and devastating against her ear, until her mouth was desperate for its return to hers.

Her mouth was to go unsatisfied. He pulled her away with the same arrogance as he had pulled her to him. Dazed and limp, she could do no more than stare up at him as her body throbbed with a myriad of newly discovered desires.

"You're learning fast, Sam. That was enough to keep any man moving through a six-foot snowdrift."

Furious, and humiliated by her own response, she drew back her hand.

"Now, Sam." He caught her wrist easily, holding it aloft, ignoring her efforts to escape. "You're not strong enough yet for wrestling. Give yourself a couple more days." Turning her hand over, his lips brushed her palm, causing her struggles to cease abruptly. "I'm going to bring in Wolfgang to keep an eye on you. Take it easy today, and try to remember, you're not as tough as you'd like to think."

Ruffling her hair as though she were a child, he disappeared into the adjoining mudroom.

Later Samantha indulged in a hot, steaming shower, attempting to forget, as she soaped her skin, the feel of Jake's hands running over her. In the bedroom, she noticed her clothes piled neatly on the spoon-back chair. She slipped them on and wandered through the house in aimless exploration, the Saint Bernard lumbering at her heels.

The house abounded in small, delightful treasures, an oak rolltop desk, a wall box with Friesian carving, a Windsor cradle. With a small sigh, she wondered if the latter had rocked the baby Jake. Opening yet another door, she found Jake's library.

It smelled of leather and age, and her fingers ran over volume after volume. She pulled out a small volume of love poetry and opened the cover. Light, feminine handwriting adorned the top corner, and her mouth turned down at the inscription.

Darling Jake . . . To remind you.
                Love, Lesley

Shutting the book with a snap, Samantha held it for one heat-blinded movement over the wastebasket, then, grinding her teeth, stuck it firmly back in place.

"It makes no difference to me," she informed Wolfgang. "She can give him a hundred books of poetry, she can give him a thousand books of poetry. It's her privilege."

She nudged the big dog with her toe. "Come on, Wolfgang, let's get moving."

She returned to the living room and built up the fire, which had burned down to a hissing pile of embers. She curled up beside it.

One hour slipped into two, two slipped into three. Surely, Jake should be home by now, she told the silent clock as the hands crept past six. It was getting dark. Rising, Samantha stared out into the diminishing light.

What if something had happened to Jake? Her throat went dry, fear creeping along her skin. Nothing could happen to him, she told herself, running her hands over her arms to combat the sudden chill. He's strong and self-reliant.

But why am I so worried about him?

"Because," she said aloud, slowly, *"I love him. I've lost my mind and fallen in love with him."* Her hands lifted to cover her eyes as the weight of the knowledge crushed down on her.

"Oh, how could I be so stupid? Of all the men in the world, I had to fall in love with this one."

A man, she remembered, *who had chosen Lesley Marshall to be his wife.* Is that why I've felt pulled in two? Is that why I responded to him when I've never responded to anyone else? Looking out into the darkness, she shuddered. I might as well admit that I don't care about anything except his getting home. . . .

When finally the sound of the outside door slamming reached her ears, she ran into the mudroom and threw herself at an astonished, snow-covered Jake.

"Sam, what's going on?" He tried to pull her away from his cold, wet jacket.

"I was afraid something had happened to you." Her voice was muffled against his chest, her cheek oblivious to the frigid dampness.

"Nothing's happened, except I'm half-frozen and soaked to the skin." Firmly now, he took her shoulders, disentangling himself from her arms. "You're getting covered with snow." His grip was gentle. She stared up at him with huge, swimming eyes. "I'm sorry I was gone so long, but things were piled up, and it's slow working in a mess like this."

Embarrassed by her outburst, she backed away. "You must be exhausted. I'm sorry, it was stupid to go on like that. It must come from being alone in the house all day." As she babbled, she was backing purposefully toward the door. "You probably want a shower and something hot to drink. I — I've got dinner on."

"Something smells good," he commented. His eyes roamed over her flushed face, and a smile spread over his features.

"S-Spaghetti," she stammered and despised herself. "I'll go finish it up."

Retreating into the kitchen, Samantha kept her back toward him when he emerged and announced casually that he would have a hot shower before dinner. She mumbled a vague reply, pretending a complete involvement with her dinner preparation. Listening to his receding footsteps, she let out a long, pent-up breath.

"Oh, idiot that I am," she sighed, and pushed her hair from her face in an angry gesture. The type of behavior she had displayed in the mudroom would only lead to trouble. She took a solemn oath to keep her emotions on a tight leash as long as Jake Tanner was around.

Tomorrow, she remembered, with a mixture of relief and disappointment, she would be back with her sister, and avoiding Jake would be a great deal easier. She had only to get through one more evening without making a fool of herself, and then she would sort out her thinking.

She was setting the table when Jake returned.

"If that tastes as good as it smells, I'll die a happy man." He lifted the lid on the pot and gave a sigh of approval. Grinning, he disappeared for a moment, then returned with a bottle of wine just as she was placing the pot on the table.

"A nice burgundy," he said, opening the bottle and setting out two glasses.

"Samantha, this is fantastic." He broke off eating long enough to give her a smile. "Where'd you learn to cook like this?"

"More of my mother's famous lessons."

"What else can you do?"

"Well, let's see. I do a rather superb swan dive, a very graceful arabesque, I can walk on my hands as easily as some walk on their feet, whip up an incredible quiche, and waltz without counting the time."

"I am suitably impressed. How did a woman of your talents spend the day?"

She sighed and grimaced and began to toy with her spaghetti. "Sleeping, mostly."

"Hmm." His cough did not quite cover his laugh.

After dinner, Samantha insisted on seeing to the washing up herself. She wanted to avoid the intimacy of working side by side with him in the confines of the kitchen.

When the last signs of the man had vanished, she walked down the hall to the living room. Jake was adding another log to the low, shifting blaze. As she entered, he turned to smile at her. "Want some brandy?"

"No, no, thank you." She took a deep breath and willed her legs to carry her to the sofa.

"Not in training, are you?" He moved from the hearth to join her on the sofa.

Smiling, she shook her head. "The fire's wonderful." Grasping the first topic that came to mind, she riveted her eyes on the flames. "I always wanted one in my apartment. We had one at home, and Bree and I used to pop corn over it. We'd always burn it, and . . ."

The rest of her rush of words was lost as Jake placed his finger under her chin and turned her face to his. His face moved closer, and when she jerked back in defense, his brow lifted in amusement. He bent toward her again, and again she started.

"I'm only going to kiss you, Samantha." His grip tightened on her chin. Sliding from her chin, his hand framed her face as his lips moved over hers, soft as a whisper. In spite of herself, she relaxed against him. Her lips parted, inviting him to explore, begging him to take.

"Samantha." Her name was a sigh.

"Kiss me again," she whispered slowly as she lifted her mouth to his.

With a low groan, he brought his lips down on hers. She clung to him, her body throbbing with heat, her heart desperate against his, while a part of her looked on, aghast, as she answered his kiss.

Her mouth clung, avid and sweet, to his. Dormant passion exploded into life until there remained only man and woman and the need, older than time, to love and be loved, to possess and be possessed.

He opened her shirt and claimed her breast. The first desperation mellowed into slow exploration as his fingers trailed lightly, drugging her with a new, delirious languor. His mouth moved to sample the taste of her neck, his face buried in the spreading lushness of her hair. She pressed against the rippling muscles of his back as his mouth and tongue and hands raged fire over her.

She felt rather than heard him say her name against her mouth, sensed rather than felt the tension enter his body before her lips were set free. Dimly, she heard the strident insistence of bells ringing as she groped to bring heaven back within reach.

"Hell of a time for them to fix the phones." She opened her eyes, dark as sapphires, and stared without comprehension. "There's nothing I'd like more than to ignore it, Samantha, but it might be important." Her lids fluttered in confusion. She could feel the warm raggedness of his breath against her cheek. "The phones have been out for two days, and there's a lot of damage out there."

His body left hers and took the warmth with it. She struggled to sit up, pulling her shirt closed. The hands that worked at the buttons were unsteady and, rising on weak legs, she sought the warmth of the fire. Pushing at tumbled hair, she wrapped her arms around her body and closed her eyes.

What had she done, losing herself that way? Tossing away pride like damaged goods! What if the phone hadn't rung? Her arms closed tighter. Does love always hurt? Does it always make a fool of you?

"Samantha." She whirled at the sound of her name, her arms still tight in protection. "It's Sabrina." Dropping her eyes from his, she moved into the hall.

Samantha picked up the phone and swallowed. "Hi, Bree." Her voice sounded strangely high-pitched to her ears, and her fingers gripped hard on the receiver.

"Sam, how are you?"

Taking a deep breath, she answered. "Fine. How *you* are is more important."

"Stronger every minute. I'm so glad you had the sense to head for the Double T when the snow started. The thought of you getting caught in that blizzard makes my blood turn cold."

"That's me, a steady head in a crisis." Samantha nearly choked on a gurgle of hysterical laughter.

"Are you sure you're all right? You sound strange. You aren't coming down with a cold, are you?"

"It's probably the connection."

"I thought they'd never get the phones fixed! I guess I just couldn't really relax until I'd talked to you and made sure you were safe! Of course, I know Jake would take care of you, but it's not the same as hearing your voice. I won't keep

100

you, Sam, we'll see you tomorrow. By the way, I think Shylock misses you."

"Probably indigestion. Tell him I'll see him tomorrow." After replacing the receiver, she stared at it for a full minute.

"Samantha." She whirled again at Jake's voice, finding him watching her from the living room archway.

"I . . . ah . . . Bree seems fine." She avoided his eyes and toyed with the ink pot by the phone. She took a step backward as Jake advanced. "She said she thought Shylock misses me. That's quite an accomplishment, he's so self-sufficient and aloof."

"Samantha. Come, sit down." He held out his hand for hers. She knew if he touched her, she would be lost.

"No, no, I think I'll go to bed, I'm still not quite myself." Her color had ebbed again, leaving pale cheeks and darkened eyes.

"Still running, Sam?" The anger in his tone was well controlled.

"No, no, I . . ."

"All right, then, for the moment we seem to be at a stalemate." He captured her chin before she could avoid the gesture. "But we haven't finished by a long shot. Do you understand?"

She nodded, then broke away to flee to the sanctuary of her room.

Chapter 8

As each day passed, Sabrina became more cheerful. Her features took on a roundness that gave her a contented appearance. And as Samantha watched her, she wondered if Sabrina possessed more strength than she had ever given her credit for. It was a sobering experience to see her usually dreamy sister grabbing life with determination and purpose while she herself couldn't seem to stop day-dreaming. Jake Tanner, she had to admit, was disturbing her days and sneaking into her dreams.

Stuffing her hands in her pockets, she scowled and continued her morning trudge to the mailbox. He meant to have her, did he? Well, Samantha Evans had no intention of being had by anyone, especially some annoying cowboy with too much charm for his own good . . . and fascinating green eyes, and that beautiful mouth. . . .

Now the days began to lengthen. The sun grew in strength. Spring began to drift over the basin greening the grass and teasing the crocuses to push their heads from the earth.

Scurrying down the hall as the doorbell interrupted her latest project — painting the nursery — Samantha wiped a few streaks of canary yellow on her jeans and opened the door.

The woman in the doorway smiled, her almond-shaped dark eyes making a thorough survey. "Hello, you must be Samantha. I'm Lesley Marshall."

The introduction was unnecessary, for with an instinct she had been unaware of possessing, Samantha had recognized the woman instantly. "Please, come in. It's still rather cold, isn't it?" She smiled, refusing to acknowledge the effort it cost her, and shut the nippy May air outside.

"I'm so glad to meet you at last." The dark eyes swept down, then up Samantha briefly. "I've heard so much about you." There was light amusement in her voice.

"Oh, really? I'm afraid I can't say the same." Her smile was faintly apologetic. "But, of course, I've been rather busy."

"I would have been by sooner, but I wanted to wait until Sabrina was more up to company."

"Bree's feeling much better these days. I'm sure she'll be glad to see you. Let me take your coat." Samantha hung the soft fur in the hall closet. Turning back to her visitor, she needed all her willpower to keep the social smile in place. The oatmeal slacks accentuated Lesley's sleekness; the trim cerise blouse set off her delicately feathered ebony hair and the perfect ivory of her skin. Desperately, Samantha wished a miracle would transform her navy sweatshirt with its Wilson High School banner and her paint-streaked jeans into something smart and sophisticated. As usual, her hair was escaping from its pins. She resisted the urge to bring her hand up to it and jam them in tightly.

"Bree's in the living room," she announced, knowing the pale gray eyes had studied her and found her wanting. "I was just about to make some tea."

Sabrina appeared at that moment, and Samantha gladly relinquished the role of hostess and escaped to the kitchen.

"So, she's beautiful," she grumbled to an unconcerned Shylock as she set the kettle on to boil. "So, she's smooth and sophisticated and makes me feel like a pile of dirty laundry." Turning, she lowered her face to his and scowled. "Who cares?" Shylock scowled back and went to sleep. Her thoughts wandered on. "I don't imagine he's ever laughed at her and patted her head as though she were a slow-witted child," she muttered as she gathered up the tea tray.

"Sabrina, you look wonderful," Lesley commented sometime later, sipping from a dainty china cup. "I'm sure having your sister with you must be very good for you. I don't have to tell you how concerned everyone has been."

"No, and I appreciate it. Sam's made everything so easy. I didn't have anything to do but sit and heal." She shot her sister an affectionate glance. "I don't know what we would have done without her these past two months."

Lesley followed her gaze. "Jake was telling me that you're a gym teacher, Samantha," she purred, managing to make this sound faintly disgusting.

"Physical education instructor," Samantha corrected, slipping into a vague southern drawl.

"And you were in the Olympics, as well. I'm sure it must have been fascinating. You don't look the sturdy, athletic type." The shrug of her shoulders was elegant, as was the small gesture of her hand. "I suppose one can never tell." Samantha gritted her teeth against a biting retort and was vastly relieved when, glancing at a slender gold watch, Lesley suddenly rose from her chair. "I must run now, Sabrina, I have a dinner engagement." Turning to Samantha, she offered a small smile. "So happy to have met you. I'm sure we'll be seeing each other again soon."

She left amidst a swirl of fur and the drifting scent of roses. Samantha sat back in the cushioned chair, relaxing for the first time in more than an hour.

"Well, what did you think of Lesley?" Sabrina questioned, shifting into a more comfortable position on the sofa.

"Very sophisticated."

"Come on, Sam." Sabrina grinned, her hands folding across the mound of her belly. "This is Bree."

"I don't know why I should have to comment, since you seem to be reading me so well. But —" her mouth curved into a rueful smile "— I suppose she's a bit smooth for my taste, and I didn't much care for the way she looked down that aristocratic nose at me."

"Actually, you really don't appear very sturdy." The observation was made with wide-eyed innocence. Samantha grimaced, pulling pins from her hair with a sharp tug until a cascade of golden brown tumbled in confusion about her shoulders.

"She'd have gotten her own back on that one if you hadn't sent me that 'Don't make a scene' look."

"Oh, well, Lesley can be nice enough when it suits her. Her father spoils her dreadfully. Her mother died when she was barely into her teens, and he transferred all his attention to Lesley. An overabundance of clothes, the best horses, and, as she grew older, cars and European tours and so on. Whatever Lesley wants, Lesley gets."

"Poor thing." The sarcasm caused her to feel spiteful and unjust. She sighed. "I suppose too much is as bad as too little. It was nice of her to come and see how you were getting along."

Sabrina's laughter floated through the room. "Sam, darling, I've never known you to be so slow." At her sister's puzzled expression, she continued. "Lesley didn't come to see me, she came to get a look at you."

"At me?" Finely etched brows disappeared under a fringe of bangs. "What for? I wouldn't think a lowly gym teacher from Philadelphia would interest Lesley Marshall."

"Any teacher who caught Jake Tanner's attention the way you have would interest Lesley. He wouldn't have gone out of his way to show just anyone around the ranch, you know."

A light color rose in Samantha's cheeks. "I think Miss Marshall's mind was put to rest after she got a good look." Her hand moved expressively down her sweatshirt and jeans. "She'd hardly see any danger here."

"Don't underestimate yourself, Sam."

"No false modesty." Samantha's sigh came from nowhere. "If a man's attracted to silk and champagne, cotton and beer are no competition. I'm cotton and beer, Bree," she murmured. Her voice trailed away with her thoughts. "I couldn't be anything else if I wanted to."

The following day, Samantha's continuing battle with her paints and brushes was interrupted by a more welcome visitor. Annie Holloway arrived at the ranch's kitchen door with a beaming smile and a chocolate cake.

"Hi." Samantha opened the door wide in welcome. "It's nice to see you again, and bearing gifts, too."

"Never like to come empty-handed," Annie announced, handing the thickly frosted cake to Samantha. "Dan always had a partiality for chocolate cake."

"Me, too." She eyed the cake hungrily. "He's not here right now, and I was just going to make some coffee. Do you suppose we could start without him?"

"Good idea." Setting herself comfortably in a chair, Annie waved a wide-palmed hand. "I reckon it wouldn't hurt for us to have a slice or two."

"Bree's taking a nap," Samantha explained as she put down the mugs of steaming coffee. "The doctor says she still has to lie down every day, but she's beginning to grumble about it a bit. Very quietly, of course."

"You're keeping an eye on her." Annie nodded and added two generous spoons of sugar to her coffee. "Dan says she's up to company now."

"Oh, yes, people have been dropping by now and again. Ah . . ." Samantha added cream to her own cup. "Lesley Marshall was by yesterday."

"I wondered how long it would be before Lesley hauled herself over to get a look at you."

"You sound like Bree." Sipping her coffee, Samantha shook her head. "I don't know why Lesley Marshall would want to meet me."

"Easy. Lesley's a mite stingy with her possessions, and she'd like to group Jake among them. She hasn't figured out yet that Jake is his own man, and all her daddy's money can't buy him for her. When my Jake picks his woman, he'll decide the time and place. He's always been an independent rascal. He was barely twenty when he lost his folks, you know." Samantha lifted her eyes to the warm brown ones. "It wasn't an easy time for him, they'd been close. They were a pair, Jake's folks, always squabbling and loving. You're a bit like her when she was a young thing." Annie smiled, her head tilting with it as Samantha remained silent. "Nobody's going to ride rough-shod over you, at least not for long. I saw that straight off. She was stubborn as a mule with two heads, and there's times, though it's been better than ten years, I still miss her."

"It must have been hard on Jake, losing his parents and having all the responsibility of the ranch when he was still so young," Samantha murmured.

"Seemed to change from boy to man over-night, just out of college and still green. 'Course," she continued, "he'd been in the saddle since childhood and what he hadn't learned about ranching from his father and that fancy college, he learned from doing. He picked up the reins of that ranch with both hands. There's not a man who works for him wouldn't wrestle a long-horned bull if he asked them to. He can fool you with that easygoing way of his, but nobody gets the better of Jake Tanner. He runs the ranch like his life, and Lesley's going to find him a hard steer to rope and brand."

"Maybe it's more the other way around," Samantha suggested. Annie's response was prevented by the appearance at the kitchen door of the man in question.

He entered with the easy familiarity of an old friend.

"Howdy, ma'am." He broke the silence with a cocky smile, removed his battered Stetson and glanced at her attire. "Been painting?"

"Obvious, isn't it?" Samantha said sharply.

"Nice colors." He helped himself to a cup of coffee. "Are you going to part with another piece of that cake?"

"Jake Tanner!" Annie exclaimed in disgust. "You should be ashamed, gobbling Dan's cake when you've got a perfectly good one of your own at home."

"Somebody else's always tastes better, Annie." He slipped off his jacket, tossing it over a hook, and grinned boyishly. "He won't miss it, anyway. I brought you and the cake over, didn't I? You're not going to begrudge me one little piece?"

"Don't waste those eyes on me, you young devil." Annie attempted to sniff and look indignant. "I'm not one of your fillies."

Jake's appearance had successfully shattered Samantha's peace of mind. After a reasonable period of politeness, she excused herself to Annie and Jake and went back to her job in the nursery.

Samantha's artistic talent was decidedly impressionistic. The floor, protected by plastic, was splotched and splattered, but the walls were coming to life with a joy of brilliant colors. Of the four walls, two were yellow and two were white, and each was trimmed with its opposite's color. On the one wall that was unbroken by door or windows, she had begun the construction of a wide, arching rainbow, carefully merging blues into pinks into greens.

Time passed, and in the quiet concentration of her work she forgot her preoccupation with Jake. Sitting on the ladder's top step, she paused, brushing the back of her hand across her cheek absently as she viewed the results.

"That's a mighty pretty sight."

She jolted, dropping the brush with a clatter, and would have fallen from the ladder had Jake's arms not gripped her waist and prevented the tumble.

"Sure spook easy," Jake commented, removing the dangerously sloshing paint bucket from her hand.

"You shouldn't come up behind a person like that," she complained. "I might have broken my neck." She wiped her hands on the legs of her jeans. "Where's Annie?"

"With your sister. She wanted to show Annie some things she's made for the baby." He set the bucket on the floor and straightened. "I didn't think they needed me."

"No, I'm sure they didn't. I need that paint, though, and the brush you made me drop." She glanced down, but his eyes remained on hers.

"I like the blue, especially that spot on your cheek," Jake said.

She rubbed at the offending area in annoyance. "If you'd just hand those things back to me, I could finish up."

"Green's nice, too," he said conversationally, and ran a finger over a long streak on her thigh. "Wilson High." His eyes lowered to the letters on her shirt. "Is that where you taught back east?"

"Yes." She shifted, uncomfortable that the name was prominent over her breasts. "Are you going to hand me my things?"

"What are your plans for tonight?" he countered easily, ignoring her request. She stared, completely thrown off balance by his unexpected question.

"I, ah, I have a lot of things to do." She searched her mind for something vital in her schedule.

"Things?" he prompted. His smile grew as his finger began to twist through a stray curl that had escaped its confines.

"Yes, things," she retorted, abandoning the attempt to elaborate. "I'm going to be very busy, and I really want to finish this room."

"I suppose I could let you get by with that, even though we both know better. Well." He smiled and shrugged. "Come down and kiss me goodbye, then. I've got to get back to work."

"I will not kiss you goodbye. . . ." she began, the words trailing off as he gripped her waist. Her hands automatically went to his arms, and he plucked her from her perch.

He lowered her slowly, his eyes never leaving hers, and her mouth was roughly claimed before her feet could reach the floor. His hands slipped under her shirt to roam the smooth skin of her back, pressing her closer as her body betrayed her and dissolved against his. Slowly he explored her soft, firm breasts, subtly rounded hips, lean thighs.

Every time, every time, her mind murmured. Every time he kisses me, I go under deeper, and one day I'll never find my way back. His teeth moved to nip at her ear and neck, searching and finding new vulnerabilities before returning to ravage her mouth again. Without will, without choice, she rested in his arms, surrendering to forces she could never defeat.

He drew her away, breaking the intimacy, but his mouth returned to hers to linger briefly before he spoke. "About tonight, Samantha."

"What?" she murmured as his tongue traced the softness of her lips.

"I want to see you tonight."

Jerking herself back into reality, she pressed her hands against his chest, but did not manage to break away. "No, no, I'm busy. I told you."

"So you did," he acknowledged, and his eyes narrowed in speculation.

His words were cut off by the sound of Sabrina's laughter drifting down the hall. Samantha wiggled against Jake's hold. "Let me go, will you?"

"Why?" He was grinning now, enjoying the flood of color in her cheeks.

"Because . . ."

"Don't ever play poker, Sam." The warning was curt. "You'd lose your shirt."

"I . . . I . . ."

"Sabrina's due in September, right?"

The sudden question caused her to blink in confusion. "Well, yes, she . . ."

"That gives you a little breathing space, Samantha." He leaned down, and his kiss was hard and brief and to the point. "After that, don't expect to get away so lightly."

"I don't know what . . ."

"You know exactly what I mean," he said interrupting. "I told you I meant to have you, and I always get what I want."

Her eyes flashed. "If you think I'm going to let you make love to me just because you say so, then you . . ."

The suggestion she would have made died as his mouth took hers again. She went rigid telling herself she would not amuse him with a response this time. As she told herself she would not, her arms circled his neck. Her body became pliant, her lips parted with the hunger she had

114

lived with all through the past month. As he took, she offered more; as he demanded, she gave. Her own mouth was mobile, her own hands seeking, until it seemed the month of fasting had never been.

"I want you, I don't have to tell you that, do I?"

She shook her head, trying to steady her breathing as his eyes alone caused her pulse to triple its rate.

"We'll settle this in September, unless you decide to come to me sooner." She began to shake her head again, but the fingers on the back of her neck halted the movement. "If you don't come to me, I'll wait until after the baby's born and you've got that much off your mind. I'm a patient man, Sam, but . . ." He stopped talking as Annie and Sabrina stepped into the room.

"Well." Annie shook her head at the two of them. "I can see he's been giving you a hard time." She turned to Sabrina with a half-exasperated shrug. "He's always been fresh as a new-laid egg. This is going to be a beautiful room, Sam." She glanced around at Samantha's handiwork, nodding in approval. "Let go of the little lady now, Jake, and take me back home, I've got dinner to fix."

"Sure. I've already said what I came to say." He released Samantha with a last, penetrating look and strode from the room, calling a goodbye over his shoulder.

"Fresh as a new-laid egg," Annie reiterated, and echoing his goodbye, followed him.

When the guests had departed, Samantha began to gather up paint buckets and brushes.

"Sam." Walking over, Sabrina placed a hand on her sister's arm. "I had no idea."

"No idea about what?" Bending, she banged the lid securely on rose pink.

"That you were in love with Jake." The truth she had avoided for so long was out in the open now: She had fallen hopelessly, irrevocably in love with Jake Tanner! Standing, Samantha searched in vain for words of denial.

"We know each other too well, Sam," Sabrina said before she could answer. "How bad is it?"

Samantha lifted her hands and let them fall to her sides. "Terminal."

"Well, what are you going to do about it?"

"Do about it?" Samantha repeated. "What can I do about it? After the baby comes, I'll go back east and try to forget about him."

"I've never known you to give up without a fight," Sabrina spoke sharply. At the unexpected tone, Samantha's brows rose.

"I'd fight for something that belonged to me, Bree, but I don't move in on someone else's territory."

"Jake's not engaged to Lesley Marshall. Nothing's official."

"I'm not interested in semantics." Samantha began to fiddle with the paint cans. "Jake wants an affair with me, but he'll marry Lesley Marshall."

"Are you afraid to compete with Lesley?" Bree asked.

Samantha whirled around, eyes flashing. "I'm not afraid of anyone," she stormed. Sabrina's lips curved in a smug smile. "Don't try your psychology on me, Sabrina! Lesley Marshall and I don't belong in the same league, but I'm not afraid of her. I *am* afraid of getting hurt, though." Her voice wavered and Sabrina's arm slipped over her shoulder.

"All right, Sam, we won't talk about it any more right now. Leave those brushes, I'll wash them out. Go take a ride. You know the only way to clear your head is to go off by yourself."

"I'm beginning to think you know me too well." With a wry smile, Samantha wiped her hands on her jeans.

"I know you, all right, Samantha." Sabrina patted her cheek and urged her from the room. "I just haven't always known what to do about you."

Chapter 9

During the months since their first meeting, Samantha had grown to know Jake Tanner, and to realize that when he wanted something, he made certain he got it. And she knew he wanted her.

If, when she rode out on horseback, she kept closer to the ranch than had been her habit, she told herself it was not fear of encountering Jake that prompted the action, but simply her desire to spend more of her free time with Sabrina. Now Sabrina was growing cumbersome in her pregnancy, there was a grain of truth to this, so Samantha found it easy to accept the half-truth.

Every day she fell more under the spell of Wyoming. Bare branches were now fully cloaked in green. The cattle grew sleek and fat. The land was fully awakened and rich.

"I think you may just have twins in there, Bree," Samantha commented as the two sisters took advantage of golden sun and fragrant warmth. Sabrina glanced down to where Samantha sat cross-legged on the wide front porch. "Dr. Gates thinks not." She patted the mound in question. "He says there's only one, and I'm just getting fat. One of us should have twins, though."

"I'm afraid that's going to be up to you, Bree. I think I'll revive the tradition of old-maid school teachers."

Sabrina was sensitive to the wistfulness in the words. "Oh, no, you'll have to get married, Sam. You can't let all those lessons go to waste."

This brought the light laugh it had intended. "I'm perfectly serious. Remember what Madame Dubois always said: 'Von must reach for ze stars.'"

"Oh, yes, Madame Dubois." Samantha smiled at the memory of their former ballet teacher. "You know, of course, that accent was a phony. She came from New Jersey."

"I'm suitably crushed. She did think she had a genuine protégé in you."

"Yes, I was magnificent." Samantha sighed with exaggerated pride.

"Let's see a few of your famous leaps now, Sam."

"Not on your life!"

"Come on, cutoffs are as good as a tutu any day. I'd join you in a pas de deux, but it would actually be a pas de trois."

Samantha rose reluctantly from her seat on the porch. "All right, I don't mind showing off a little."

With quiet dignity, Sabrina began to hum a

movement from *Swan Lake*, and Samantha lowered into a purposefully dramatic body sweep before exploding with an energetic series of grand jetés, stage leaps and cabrioles. She concluded the performance with a group of pirouettes, ended by dropping in a dizzy heap on the grass.

"That's what you get," she said, closing her eyes and shaking her head at the giddiness, "when you forget to spot focus."

"Is this show open to the public?"

Samantha glanced sharply toward the sound of the all-too-familiar voice.

"Dan!" Sabrina exclaimed. "I didn't expect you back so early."

"Ran into Lesley and Jake out on the north boundary," he explained, striding over and planting a firm kiss. "I thought you and Sam might like some company."

"Hello, Lesley, Jake." Sabrina included them both in her smile. "Have a seat, I'll bring out something cool."

Samantha had been sitting, praying without result for the ground to open up and swallow her. "I'll do it, Bree." She jumped at the opportunity to escape. "Don't get up."

"I'm up," Sabrina pointed out, disappearing inside before Samantha could argue.

"Do you teach ballet, as well, Samantha?" Lesley asked. She surveyed Samantha's outfit of semi-ragged cutoffs and T-shirt with dark, mocking eyes.

"No, no," Samantha muttered, feeling once more desperately at a disadvantage next to the slim woman in elegantly tailored breeches and silk shirt.

"I thought it was real nice," Dan commented, innocently turning the knife.

"Samantha's just full of surprises," Jake said.

Now that he had spoken again, Samantha was forced to give Jake a portion of her attention. He looked devastatingly male, the denim shirt rolled past his elbows to expose bronzed, corded arms, the low-slung belt in his jeans accentuating his leanness. She concentrated on a spot approximately six inches to the left of his face, in order to avoid the smile that had already mastered his face.

"Yeah," she returned. "I'm just a bushel of surprises."

"Anything you can't do, Sam?"

"A few things." She attempted a cool sophistication.

"You're so energetic," Lesley commented, slipping her hand through Jake's arm. "You must be horribly strong and full of bulging muscles."

For one heady moment, Samantha considered flight. She was opening her mouth to make her excuses when Dan effectively cut off all hope.

"Sit down, Sam, I want to talk over a little idea with you and Sabrina." Sinking down on the porch steps, Samantha avoided any glimpse of Jake's face. "Do you think Sabrina's up to a little party?" Samantha looked up at Dan's question and attempted to marshal her thoughts.

"A party?" she repeated, drawing her brows together in concentration. "I suppose so. Dr. Gates says she's doing very well, but you could always ask to be sure. Did you want to go to a party?"

"I was thinking of having one," he corrected with a grin. "There're these twins I know who have this birthday in a couple of weeks." Bending over, he tugged at Samantha's loosened locks. "Seems like a good excuse for having a party."

"Oh, our birthday." Samantha's response was vague. The impending anniversary had slipped her mind.

"Did I hear someone say party?" Sabrina emerged through the screen door with a tray of iced tea.

Samantha sipped the cool, sweet tea her sister handed her and watched Sabrina's face light up with anticipation.

"A birthday party, Sam." She turned to her sister, eyes shining with excitement. "When's the last time we had one?"

"When we were twelve and Billy Darcy got sick all over Mom's new carpet." Leaning back against the porch rail, Samantha unwittingly lifted her face to Jake's.

"Well, then, it's high time for another," Dan said. "What do you say, Sam? I know it means extra work for you."

"Huh." Tearing her eyes from Jake's smile, she endeavored to pick up the threads of the conversation. "What? Oh, no, it's no trouble. It'll be fun." Concentrating on Dan's face, she blocked out the sight of Lesley lounging intimately against Jake. "How many people did you have in mind?"

"Just neighbors and friends." He reached up to rub his chin. "About thirty or forty, I'd say. What do you think, Lesley?"

The full mouth pouted a moment in thought. "If you want to keep it small, Dan," she agreed after a short deliberation. Samantha's eyes grew wide. These people definitely had a different idea of small than she did.

"Oh, Lesley, come take a look at this punch bowl I've got, see if you think we should use it." Rising, Sabrina took Dan's hand. "Come, get it down for me, Dan." Throwing her sister an innocent smile, Sabrina disappeared inside and left her alone with Jake.

"How's the painting coming?" Jake stretched both arms over the back of the swing.

"Painting? Oh, the nursery. It's finished."

That, she recalled with a frown, was just one of many times he had come upon her in a ridiculous situation. Sleeping on stumps, covered with paint, and now leaping across the lawn like some crazed ballerina. Samantha, she told herself, you have class.

"What do you want for your birthday, Sam?" He prodded her with the toes of his boot and earned a scowl.

Blowing a wisp of hair from her eyes, she moved her shoulders. "Fur, diamonds."

"No, you're not the type for furs." Taking out a cigar, he lit it and blew a lazy stream of smoke. "You'd be thinking about all the little minks that were scalped to make it. And diamonds wouldn't suit you."

"I suppose I'm more the quartz type." She rose, irritated.

"No, I was thinking more of sapphires." He caught her wrist. "To go with your eyes, or maybe rubies to go with your temper."

"I'll be sure to put both on my list. Now, if you'll excuse me." She glanced at her captured hand, then back at him. "I've got to go feed my cat." She gestured to where Shylock lay on the far side of the porch.

"He doesn't look very hungry."

"He's pretending to be dead," she muttered. "Shylock, let's eat."

Amber eyes opened and blinked. Then, to her pleasure, Shylock rose and padded toward her. However, upon reaching his mistress, he gave her a disinterested stare, leaped into Jake's lap and began to purr with wicked enjoyment.

"No, ma'am." Jake glanced down at the contented cat. "He doesn't look hungry at all."

With a final glare, Samantha turned, stalked to the door and slammed the screen smartly behind her.

The sun shone warm and friendly on the morning of the twins' birthday. Samantha carried a large parcel into the kitchen. Dumping her burden on the table where her sister was enjoying a cup of tea, she nudged Shylock away with her foot. She had not yet decided to forgive him for his treacherous advances to Jake.

"This just came, it's from the folks."

"Open it, Sam." Sabrina poked an experimental finger at the package. "Dan refuses to give me my present yet, and I've searched everywhere I can think of."

"I bet it's six books on child rearing for you, and six on etiquette for me."

"A present's a present," Sabrina stated, and tore the mailing paper from the box.

"Here's a note." After breaking the seal, Samantha produced a sheet of paper and read aloud.

"To Samantha and Sabrina:

A very happy birthday and our love to you both. Sabrina, I do hope you are taking good care of yourself. As you know, proper diet and rest are essential. I'm sure having Samantha with you during the last weeks of your confinement is a great comfort. Samantha, do look after your sister and see that she takes the necessary precautions. However, I hope you're not overlooking your own social life. As your mother, it is my duty to remind you that you are long past the marriageable age. Your father and I are looking forward to seeing you and our first grandchild in a few weeks. We will be in Wyoming the first part of September, if Dad's schedule holds true.

With love,
Mom and Dad

"There's a postscript for you, Bree.

"Sabrina, doesn't Daniel know any suitable men for your sister?"

With a sigh, Samantha folded the letter and dropped it on the table. "She never changes." Dipping into the box, Samantha plucked out a smaller one with Sabrina's name on it and handed it to her. "Marriageable age," she muttered, and shook her head.

"Did you peek in here before?" Sabrina accused, dumping out volumes on infant and child care.

"No," Samantha denied with a superior smirk. "I just know Mom." Drawing out her own package, she ripped off the concealing paper. "Good grief." She let the box drop to the table and held up a brief black lace negligee.

"I thought I knew Mom." Both sisters burst into laughter. "She must be getting desperate," Samantha concluded, holding the negligee in front of her.

"Now that's a pretty thing," Jake observed as he and Dan entered the kitchen. "But it's

126

even prettier with something in it." Samantha bundled the garment behind her and flushed scarlet.

"Presents from Mom and Dad," Sabrina explained, indicating her stack of books.

"Very suitable." Dan grinned as he glanced through the volumes.

"Doesn't look like Sam feels the same about hers." Jake smiled. Samantha felt her already alarming color deepen. "Let's see it again."

"Don't tease, Jake." Sabrina turned to her husband. "Mom says they'll be here the first part of September."

"I'll put this stuff away." Samantha tossed the gown into the box and began to bury it under books.

"Leave that till later." Dan took her hand and pulled her away. "I need you outside for a minute."

She went willingly. Escape was escape. Imagining it had something to do with Sabrina's gift, she was surprised when Dan slowed his pace and allowed his wife to join them in their walk toward the ranch buildings. He kept her involved in a running conversation about the party until they came to a halt at the paddock fence.

"Happy birthday, Sam." Sabrina kissed her sister's cheek as Samantha's eyes focused on the golden Arabian mare.

"Oh." She could manage no more.

"She's from a good line," Dan informed her,

his arm slipping around Sabrina's shoulders. "She's out of the Double T stock, no finer in Wyoming."

"But I . . ." Words faltered, and she swallowed and tried to begin again.

"What do you give someone who packs their own life away for six months without hesitation, without asking for anything in return?" Dan's free arm slipped around Samantha and pulled her to his side.

"We figured if you insisted on going back east, we'd always have a hold on you. You'd have to come visit us to ride your mare."

"I don't know how to thank you."

"Then don't," Dan ordered. "Go try her out."

"Now?"

"Now's as good a time as any." Not needing a second urging, Samantha was over the fence, stroking the mare and murmuring.

"We may convince her to stay yet," Dan commented, watching as she slipped into the saddle and took the mare around the paddock. "I could have a word with Jake."

Sabrina shook her head. "No, Sam would be furious if we interfered. She'd bolt back to Philadelphia before we could take a breath. For now, we'd better keep out of it." She lowered her voice as a beaming Samantha trotted around to them and slipped off the little mare.

"She's a real beauty," she sighed. "I don't know how I can ever bear to leave her . . ."

Sabrina's eyes met her husband's in silent satisfaction. Perhaps it will not be necessary, their unspoken message said.

"Come, little sister," Dan said. "If you can tear yourself away from your new friend, I sure could use a cup of coffee now."

As the trio trooped back toward the house, Jake swung through the back door. "Delivery just came. It's in the living room."

"Oh," Dan murmured, looking entirely too innocent. "Come on, Sabrina, we'd best see what it is."

"Is it the piano?" Sam asked Jake, and Dan and Sabrina disappeared inside.

"Looked like one to me. I guess that's another present that'll go over big. Walk to the truck with me," Jake commanded, and captured her hand before she could protest.

"Really, Jake, I have a million things to do." She trotted to keep pace with his loose, lanky stride.

"I know, you're indispensable." Stopping by his truck, he reached in the cab and produced a package. "But this seems to be the time for gift giving. I thought I'd let you have your present now."

"You didn't have to get me anything."

"Samantha." His drawl was lazy, but his eyes narrowed in annoyance. "I never do anything unless I want to." Taking her hand from behind her back, he placed the box in it. "Open it."

Lifting the statue from its tissue bedding, she examined it in silent amazement. The alabaster was smooth and cool in her hands, carved into the shape of a horse and rider in full gallop. The artist had captured the fluid grace, the freedom of motion. She ran a hesitant finger over the delicate features.

"It looks like me." She lifted her eyes to Jake's.

"And so it should," he answered easily. "It's supposed to be you."

"But how?" She shook her head, torn between pleasure and confusion.

"A man I know does this kind of thing. I described you to him."

For the second time that day, Samantha found herself at a loss for words.

"Why?" The question was out before she could swallow it.

Slowly, a smile drifted across his face. He pushed back his hat. "Because it suits you better than furs and diamonds."

She braced herself to meet his eyes again. "Thank you."

He nodded, his face solemn. He took the box from her hands and placed it on the hood of the truck. "I think a birthday kiss is traditional."

Swallowing, she took an instinctive step in retreat, but he gripped her arms and held her still. She offered her cheek, and his laughter broke out, full and rich on the summer air. "Sam," he turned her face to his, and his eyes sparkled with humor, "you're incredible."

His lips met hers. His hand moved from her

arms to her hips, drawing her firmly against the hard lines of his body. She submitted to the embrace, as long as his arms held her, as long as they were mouth to mouth, as long as the heat from his body infused hers, he owned her, and she could not run.

Finally he drew her away, bringing his hands to her shoulders while hers rested on his chest for support.

"Happy birthday, Sam."

"Thank you," she managed, still breathless from the impact of his embrace.

He lifted the box from the hood of the truck and placed it in her hands before sliding into the cab. "See you tonight." With a salute, he started the engine. The truck moved down the road, leaving her staring after it.

Chapter 10

Party sounds filled the house. Laughter and voices and music mingled and drifted through open windows to float on the night air.

On this evening, the twins were dramatically different in their appearance. Sabrina's pale blue gown floated around her, cunningly disguising her pregnancy. Her hair was a glinting halo around rose-tinted cheeks. Samantha's black-striped satin clung to her body, her halter neckline plunging deep to a wide, gathered waist. Her hair was free and thick around her shoulders.

As she moved and mingled with the crowd, Samantha searched for a tall, lanky form, noting with increasing despair and a gnawing jealousy that a slim, dark woman had also as yet failed to put in an appearance.

Cornered by an enthusiastic young cowboy, Samantha was feeling her attention begin to wander from a detailed account of horse breeding when her eyes met dark jade across the room.

He was standing with two men she did not recognize, and Lesley Marshall stood beside him. She was elegant in an oyster-white gown. Her fine-boned ivory hand was placed from time to time on Jake's arm, as if, Samantha thought grimly, she were flaunting her possession.

Furious with the sudden feeling of inadequacy, Samantha turned to her companion with a dazzling smile. He stammered over his lecture, his words grinding to a halt. She tucked her arm in his and used her eyes without shame.

"Howdy, Tim." Jake appeared from nowhere and placed a hand on the young man's shoulder. "I'm going to steal this little lady for a moment." He paused and smiled easily into Samantha's mutinous face. "There's a couple of people she hasn't met yet."

Without waiting for an assent, he had her unwilling hand in his, propelling her through the crowd. "Tim won't be the same for weeks," he whispered close to her ear. "A woman could get run out of town for using her eyes that way on susceptible young boys," he warned, pulling her through the sea of people.

"You don't have to drag me."

"I know a stubborn mule when I see one," he countered, without bothering to lower his voice. Her furious retort was swallowed as Jake presented her to the two men who flanked Lesley.

"Sam, I'd like you to meet George Marshall, Lesley's father." Samantha's hand was enveloped in a hearty grip. "And Jim Bailey," he continued, nodding toward the second man.

"Jim only works with cattle on paper. He's a lawyer."

"My, this is a mighty pretty girl!" George Marshall boomed. Giving Jake a sly wink, he patted his daughter's shoulder.

"You always manage to rope in the pick of the herd, don't you, Jake?"

Jake slipped his hands easily into his pockets. "I do my best. But then, roping them's one thing, getting them's another."

"Well, now, little lady," George's genial voice continued, "Les tells me you're a gym teacher."

"That's right, Mr. Marshall."

"Now, you just call me George," he instructed, squeezing her shoulder with a genial affection. "Tell me, why isn't a pretty little thing like you married and settled down instead of running around some gymnasium?"

Jake was grinning with obvious enjoyment. Samantha tossed her hair behind her back, but before she could think of a suitable answer, George's laughter boomed through the room.

"I like this girl," George announced to the group. "Looks like she has spirit. You come over to our ranch any time, little lady, any time at all."

In spite of herself, Samantha found herself liking his expansive hospitality. "If you'll excuse me now, I've got . . . got to get a tray out of the kitchen." She gave the group an all-encompassing smile and melted into the crowd.

In the kitchen, she pulled a tray from the refrigerator to give her excuse credibility and was glad she had when Jake followed her in a moment later.

"George is a good man. He has the right ideas when it comes to women." Smiling knowingly at her, he leaned against the door watching her every move.

"That's your opinion," she returned tartly, bustling around the kitchen in an attempt to ignore him.

"Sit down a minute, Sam."

She glanced up, immediately wary, then lifted the tray as a defense. "No, I've got to get back."

"Please."

Despite herself, she lowered the tray to the table and herself into a chair.

"I ran into Jack Abbot, the school principal, the other day."

"Oh?"

"He told me the girls' phys ed. instructor isn't coming back next term." Leaning back in his chair, Jake studied her. "He's going to offer you the job."

"Oh," she repeated before she could stop herself.

"He wants you pretty bad. He really needs someone this fall. I told him I'd be seeing you, and that I'd mention it. He's going to call you officially, of course."

How simple, Samantha thought.

How simple it would all be if I didn't love this man. I could stay where I want to stay, work where I want to work. But now, I've got to refuse, I've got to go away.

"I appreciate your telling me, and I appreciate Mr. Abbot wanting me, but . . . ."

"Don't appreciate it, Samantha, think about it."

"You don't know what you're asking me to do."

He rose to pace the room, his hands seeking the depths of his pockets. "I'm just asking you to think about it. You like it here. You've made friends. You like being near your sister. You'd still have the satisfaction of doing what you feel you're suited for. Is it so much to ask that you consider it?"

"Yes, it's quite a lot. Jake, I don't want to argue with you. There are things I have to do, the same way there are things you have to do."

"All right." He nodded, then repeated slowly, as if coming to a decision. "All right, there *are* things I have to do." Moving over, he captured her chin between his thumb and fingers.

His arms slipped around her waist to bring her close, his mouth lowering to brush her cheeks and the corners of her lips. "Come home with me now, Samantha. We can be alone there." His voice had become low and seductive, as his fingers trailed over the bare skin of her back.

"No, please don't." She turned her face away.

"I want to make love to you. I want to feel your skin under my hands, all of you. I want to hear you sigh when I touch you."

"Jake, please." She dropped her head to his chest. "It's unfair, here, like this."

"Then come home with me."

"No, I can't." She shook her head without raising it. "I won't."

"All right, Samantha." He framed her face and brought it up to his. "I said I'd give you until the baby was born. We'll stick to that. We won't argue tonight. Let's call it a truce for your birthday. Agreed?"

He kissed her once, briefly, and turned to lift the tray. "Then we'll both do what we have to do when the time comes."

Leaving her confused, Jake moved through the doorway.

Rejoining the festivities, Samantha moved from group to group, but her thoughts were only about Jake. Why was he so interested in her career choices? Why did he want her to take the job in Wyoming? *Maybe he cared for her.* For a brief moment, she allowed hope to shimmer. Her eyes swept the room to find him. Finally she spotted him. He was dancing with Lesley. The shining cap of her raven hair brushing his cheek, the ivory of her hand entwined with the bronze of his. Samantha winced as he threw back his head and laughed at something Lesley had said for his ears alone.

Care for me? her mind repeated in a scathing whisper. Grow up, Samantha, *caring* and *wanting* don't always mean the same thing. In a few weeks, she comforted herself, she would no longer be subjected to this constant pain. When the ache had eased, she could visit Bree again. Jake would probably be too busy with his wife to spare time for visits to the Lazy L. Samantha felt her heart contract with pain.

She turned away and bumped solidly into Jim Bailey.

"Sorry." He took her shoulders to steady her. "I didn't see you."

"It's all right," she returned, offering a smile. "Besides, I think I ran into you."

"Well, no harm done either way." She watched his eyes slide past her and focus on Jake and Lesley. "They look nice together, don't they?"

Embarrassed that he must have seen her staring at them, Samantha nodded, and looked down at her empty glass. "Come on, we better get you a refill."

A few moments later, they joined the group around the piano as Sabrina played.

"So, you're a lawyer." She smiled at Jim. "I don't think I've ever met a lawyer before."

Jim returned her smile. "And you're a gymnast."

"No, actually, I'm a gym teacher now."

He lifted his glass in a toast and drank. "I remember you. I've always been an avid fan of the Olympics. I thought you were fabulous."

"Well, that's nice to hear after a decade."

He tapped his glass to hers. "Well, Olympic star, would you like to dance?"

"I'd love to."

Samantha enjoyed Jim Bailey's easy conversation. She learned during their two dances that he was interested in getting into politics. His dark good looks and ready wit would certainly be assets, she decided.

"Sam." Sabrina motioned to her as they moved back toward the piano. "It's your turn. Union rules."

"Okay," Samantha agreed, sliding onto the bench.

She played with practiced ease, moving from one song to the next. Time slipped through her fingers. As in a dream, she was aware of the voices behind her, the faint, drifting breeze of Wyoming through the opened windows.

Someone sat beside her. Recognizing the lean fingers that lifted to turn the page of her sheet music, she faltered and missed a note.

"You and Jim seem to have hit it off." Samantha heard the click of his lighter over the sounds of the party.

"He's a very nice man. Have you known him long?"

"Oh, only since we were about eight and I gave him a black eye and he loosened a few of my teeth."

"Sounds like a loving friendship."

Jake again turned the page before she could

do so herself. "Well, after that we sort of stuck together." He pushed the curtain of hair behind her shoulder, and Samantha struggled not to break the thread of the melody. "The two of you seemed to have a lot to talk about."

"He's very charming, and we have a few mutual interests."

"Hmm." Jake shifted slightly in his seat. His thigh brushed hers, and her fingers responded by hitting three wrong notes.

"You play very well."

Was he being ironic? She turned to look at him, but found no mockery in his jade eyes.

"Pleasantly," she corrected. "I get the general melody, but the details are a bit fuzzy."

"I've noticed that you have a tendency to shrug off your own capabilities. Are you aware of that?"

"That's not true. I just know what I do well and what I don't."

"You're a very tough critic, and you're inclined to underestimate."

"Honesty," she countered, finishing the song with a flourish. "I am a totally honest person."

"Are you, Samantha?" he said softly. "That's what I plan to find out."

Chapter 11

The days grew hot and sultry. The skies were improbably blue, rarely softened by clouds.

Long hours in the sun had deepened the honey of Samantha's skin, teasing out the gold in her hair. As long as she was occupied, she had no time for soul searching. She could enjoy the long summer days without thinking of the fall. As Sabrina wilted like a thirsty rose in the searing heat, Samantha confined her own activities to the early-morning hours. In the long, hot haze of the afternoon, Sabrina moved slowly through the house, her body clumsy. Samantha did not dare leave her. The baby was due in two weeks, and Samantha wanted to remain within calling distance of her sister as much as possible.

One particularly humid afternoon, the two women were sitting idly in the living room. Sabrina got up heavily from her chair to look out the window. "Sam," she said, "before Dan left for town, he said a storm was brewing. From the looks of the sky, I'd say he was right."

Before Samantha could answer, there was a

sudden flash of lightning. A blast of thunder rolled in on the wind, and the rain began to fall in sheets.

"It's coming down fast," Samantha agreed. "It should cool us off a bit." She looked sympathetically at her sister's bulky form.

The storm built in power. Jagged flashes of lightning illuminated the room and an angry wind hurled the rain against the windows. The two women watched in fascination as the storm exhausted itself. Soon rain dripped tentatively from the eaves and the thunder was a mere grumble in the distance.

The sun struggled to reappear, breaking through the gloom with a hazy promise of light.

"That," Sabrina commented with an enormous sigh, "was a mean one."

Samantha turned from her place by the window and again slumped into a chair. "Remember when you used to hide in the closet whenever we had a thunderstorm?"

"All too well." She gave her sister a pained smile. "And you used to stand on the porch, loving every minute of it, until Mom dragged you in, soaking wet. On that note from the past," Sabrina announced, and struggled to her feet, "I'm going to take a nap, Sam." She turned at the doorway and studied the woman slouched in the chair, bare legs and feet stretched out in unconscious grace. "I love you."

With a rather puzzled smile, Samantha watched her walk away.

Wandering out to the porch, Samantha drank in the rain-fresh air. Everything sparkled. Raindrops clung like jewels to blossoms and leaves. Though the flowers had drooped with the weight of the storm, their colors had been washed into brilliant life. A bird, flying by on a shaft of light, trilled above her. She could hear the steady dripping of the rain off the eaves above the whisper of the dying wind. Satisfied, she curled up on a porch rocker and instantly fell asleep.

She had no idea how long she had drifted in the soft twilight world when, with reluctance, she woke at the touch of a hand on her shoulder. She looked up drowsily and yawned. "Oh, Bree, I must have fallen asleep. It's so wonderfully cool out here."

"Sam, I think the baby's decided to put in an unscheduled appearance."

"Huh? Oh!" Springing to her feet, she was instantly awake. "Right now? Dan's not here, and it's not time yet. Sit down, sit," she ordered, running agitated fingers through her hair.

"I think the first thing to do is to calm down," Sabrina suggested.

"You're right. I'm not going to fall apart, it was just a shock. I wasn't expecting this for another week or two."

"Neither was I." Sabrina's smile was half amused, half apologetic.

"All right, how long have you been having contractions, and how far apart are they?"

"Only for an hour or so."

"That should give us plenty of time." Samantha patted Sabrina's hand.

"But they've been getting awfully strong, and . . ." Breaking off, she closed her eyes and began to breathe in a deep, methodical rhythm. "And," she continued, after a final long breath, "awfully close together."

"How close?" Samantha asked, feeling new tension at the base of her neck.

"Ten minutes."

"Ten minutes," Samantha repeated. "I'd better get you to the hospital. I'll bring the car around. Stay put," she told her sister, and raced to the garage.

Upon reaching Sabrina's compact and sliding behind the wheel, Samantha was horrified to find the engine unresponsive to the turn of the key. The little car sputtered, emitted an apologetic groan and died.

"You can't," she insisted, and smacked the steering wheel. "We just had you fixed."

There was no use wasting more time trying to figure out what was wrong with the car. It was clearly not going to start, and Samantha hadn't the first idea of where to look for the problem.

Rushing back to the house, she picked up the phone in the kitchen. At least she could call Dr. Gates. A groan of despair was wrenched from her when she heard the dead silence on the line. Oh, no, the storm must have knocked out the phones!

Forcing herself to appear calm, she returned to the living room where Sabrina was waiting for her.

Reaching her sister again, Samantha knelt down so their eyes were level. "Bree, the car won't start. All the trucks and jeeps are out with the men, and the storm must have knocked down the phone lines."

"Looks like we've got a few problems." Sabrina took a deep breath.

"It's going to be all right." Samantha took her hand in reassurance. "I'll help you get into bed, and then I'll take a horse and ride toward the Double T. If I don't see any of the men on the way, I'll get a truck there and bring it back. Most of them have radios, and I can call ahead to the doctor."

"Sam, it's going to take time for you to get there, and to get back. I don't think I'll make it in time to get to the hospital after that. You'll have to have the doctor come here."

"Here?" Samantha repeated. Her throat closed on the word. Sabrina nodded. "All right. Don't worry, I won't be long. I'll be back as soon as I can." Samantha raced off to the stables, and without wasting the time for a saddle, she leaped on her mare's back.

The familiar landscape was a blur, as she urged more speed out of the powerful horse. The sound of her own breath was masked by the sound of thudding hooves. Every minute she took was a minute longer that Sabrina was alone. She crouched lower on the horse and dug in bare heels.

When Samantha spotted the men on horseback, she spurred the Arabian over the fence in a fluid leap. As her hooves touched earth, she met the horse's sides again. They streaked across the field, scattering annoyed cattle.

When she reached the group, she reined in sharply. The mare reared, nearly unseating her. Her breath came in gasps as she struggled to keep her seat.

"What are you trying to do, break your neck?" Furiously Jake snatched the reins from her hands. "If you're stupid enough not to care about yourself, think of your horse. What do you mean riding like a fool and jumping fences? Where's your saddle? Have you lost your mind?"

"Bree," she managed at last between giant gulps of air. "The baby's coming, and the phone's out. The car wouldn't start, and there's nobody around. Dan's in town. Bree says there's no time to get her into the hospital now, and I have to call the doctor." She felt tears of fear burning at her eyes and bit her lip.

"All right, take it easy." Twisting in the saddle, Jake called out to one of his men. "Get back to the ranch and get hold of Dr. Gates on the CB radio. Tell him Sabrina Lomax is in labor and to get to the Lazy L in a hurry." Turning back, he handed the reins to Samantha. "Let's go."

"Are you coming back with me?" Flooded with relief, she gripped tight on the leather.

"What do you think?"

Together, they sprang forward in a gallop.

Speed and thundering hooves were all Samantha ever remembered of the ride back. There was no time for conversation, no time for thought. She was sliding to the ground before she came to a full stop and Jake once more secured her reins.

"Keep your head, Samantha," he ordered, watching her bound up the steps and through the front door.

The house was silent. Her stomach tightened as she rushed to the master bedroom. Sabrina sat up in bed, propped by a mound of pillows and greeted her with a cheerful smile.

"That was quick, did you fly?"

"Just about," Samantha returned, faint with relief.

"We've sent for the doctor. Everything's under control." She sat down on the bed, taking her sister's hand. "How are you doing?"

"Not too bad." Her hand closed over Samantha's, as much to reassure as seeking reassurance. "I'm glad you're back. Here comes another one."

Samantha looked on with unfamiliar helplessness. Her fingers grew tighter over her twin's, as if to steal some of her pain.

"We can thank Mom for that book on natural childbirth." Sabrina gave a long, shaky sigh and relaxed against the pillows.

"Don't look so worried, I'm doing fine. Oh,

hello, Jake." Glancing at the doorway, Sabrina greeted him with friendly cheerfulness. "I didn't know you were here. Come in. It's not contagious."

He advanced into the room, looking tall, male and out of place. His hands retreated to his pockets. "How're you doing?"

"Oh, well, you've seen a cow in labor before, I don't imagine there's much difference." The small hand tightened on Samantha's. "Here we go again."

Samantha lifted the hand to her cheek. *Where was the doctor?* Sabrina should be in the hospital, surrounded by experts.

"This baby's in a big hurry," Sabrina announced with a small moan. "I'm sorry, Sam, it's not going to wait much longer."

I don't know anything about childbirth, Samantha thought in a moment of terror. *What am I going to do? What do I do first?*

Standing, she turned to Jake. "Go sterilize some towels, lots of them, and some string and scissors."

"All right." His hand rested on her shoulder a moment. "If you need me, give a call."

Nodding, she moved into the adjoining bath and scrubbed her hands and arms until they hurt.

"You're going to be fine," she stated as she re-entered the bedroom.

"Yes, I am." Sabrina lay back on the pillows and closed her eyes. "I'm going to have this baby, Sam, and I'm going to do a good job of it. You can't do this for me, I have to be strong."

"You are strong." Brushing away the hair from Sabrina's cheeks, she realized with a sudden jolt that it was true. "You're stronger than I ever knew."

Her calm had returned, and she took over the duties of midwifery with an instinct as old as time. She wiped moisture from her sister's face, working with her, breathing with her, uttering soothing encouragements. Sabrina had not gone through all she had to lose now, and Samantha would not allow anything to go wrong.

"All right." Wiping beads of sweat from her own brow, Samantha straightened. "I think she's going to come this time, it's almost over. You have to help."

Sabrina nodded, her face pale and composed. Her hair had darkened with dampness. She shuddered and moaned with the final pang of childbirth. A thin, shrill cry pierced the stillness of the room. Samantha held new life in her hands.

"Oh, Bree." She stared down at the tiny, wriggling form.

Dan burst into the room two steps ahead of the the doctor.

Suddenly, it was all so simple, Dan standing by Sabrina's side, his large hand clutching hers, the small, fresh form swaddled in the curve of her mother's arms.

149

"Only one." Sabrina sighed, her eyes luminous. "You'll have to handle the twins, Sam. One at a time is enough for me."

Sometime later, Samantha shut the door behind her and walked toward the kitchen. Jake looked up at her approach.

"A girl." She lowered herself into a chair. "The doctor says she's perfect, almost seven pounds. Bree's fine." She pushed at her tumbled hair and ran a hand across her brow. "I want to thank you."

"I didn't do anything."

"You were here." She lifted her eyes, and they were young and vulnerable. "I needed to know you were here."

"Samantha." He smiled and shook his head. "You sure find a man's weak points. I'll get you a drink."

He was back in a moment with a decanter of brandy and two snifters. Sitting across from her, he filled both generously. "It's not champagne, but it'll do." Lifting his glass, he touched it solemnly to hers. "To mother and child, and to Samantha Evans." He paused, his smile fading into seriousness. "She's one hell of a woman."

Samantha folded her arms on the table, laid her head on them and burst into tears.

"I was so scared." She found her voice muffled against his shoulder as he brought her against him. "I've never been so scared. I thought I would lose them both."

150

He tilted her chin as one hand rubbed the small of her back. "You're a survivor, Sam, and too stubborn to let anything happen to Sabrina or the baby."

Her forehead dropped to his chest as she struggled to stem the flow of tears.

"I always seem to fall apart in front of you."

"Don't much care for that, do you?" She felt his lips descend to her hair and allowed herself the joy of being cradled in his arms. "Most people don't look for perfection, Sam, they find it boring. You," he said, framing her face with his hands, "are never boring."

She sniffed and smiled. "I guess that was a compliment." Giving in to impulse, she leaned over and rested her cheek against his. "I don't think you're boring, either."

"Well." He stroked her hair a moment, and his voice was curiously soft. "That's about the nicest thing you've ever said to me.

"Now drink some of that." He pushed her gently away and handed her the brandy.

Obeying, she allowed the warm strength to seep into her veins and relaxed with a sigh. "Bree certainly came through this better than I did." She drank again. Jake straddled a chair, leaning his arms on the back. "When I left her, she was lying there with the baby, looking like she'd just finished having a picnic. Dan looked like he was about to keel over, I was ready for someone to cart me away. Yet Bree lies there, glowing like a rose."

"Your sister's quite a woman."

151

"I know." Her eyes dropped to the surface of the table. "She said she has someone to depend on her now. I guess the time's come to stop playing big sister. She doesn't need that anymore."

"So, what will you do now?" His voice was casual.

"I'll stay around a couple of weeks, then I'll go on." She struggled, seeing only a void.

"To what?"

Her fingers tightened on her glass. "To my work, to my life." She drank, and the brandy was bitter.

"Still set on leaving?" He lifted his own glass, swirling the liquid. Amber danced under the kitchen light. "You haven't seen Wyoming in the autumn."

"No, I haven't," she answered, evading his prior question. "Maybe I'll come back next year." She stared down at her hands, knowing she never would.

"She's hungry!" Dan charged into the kitchen, his grin threatening to split his face. "Just had a baby, and she says she's hungry. Sam, I love you." Plucking her from her chair, Dan tossed her into the air. Her laughter ended on a shriek as she clutched at him on her journey down. The shriek was strangled as she was smothered by a bear hug. "I swear, if bigamy wasn't against the law, I'd marry you."

"If I was still all in one piece," she managed, turning her face and gulping for air.

"I ask you, Jake." He consulted the other man as his arms threatened to destroy the alignment of Samantha's rib cage. "Have you ever known another like this one?"

"Can't say that I have." She heard the smile in his voice, though it was impossible in her position to see his face. "I'd say Samantha is unique. One of a kind."

Rising, he lifted his brandy and toasted them both.

Chapter 12

"Sam, you're going to spoil her."

"Impossible." Sitting in the front porch rocker with the week-old Jennifer, Samantha smiled at her sister. "She's much too intelligent to be spoiled. Anyway, it's an aunt's privilege."

As she continued to rock, her lips strayed to Jennifer's soft tuft of dark hair. I won't be able to do this much longer. She looked to the massive peaks gleaming silver-blue in the afternoon sun. A light breeze stirred the air, bringing the sweet scent of freshly mowed grass. She breathed it in, and the soft scent of Jennifer's talc mingled with it. A sigh escaped.

She had not realized such a small creature could wrap her way around the heart so completely. Another love to leave behind. In just a week, I'll have to say goodbye to all the things that matter: Bree, Dan, Wyoming, and now Jennifer.

Dents and bruises, she thought again, but not the open wound that comes from leaving the man. Arrogant and gentle, demanding and kind, hot-tempered and easy; the parts that made up Jake Tanner were complicated and many, but to Samantha, it was a simple equation of love.

Blast you, Jake Tanner, if it weren't for you, I could stay. I belong here. I felt it from the first time I saw the mountains. There's nothing for me in Philadelphia. You've left me without anything to go back to.

"Looks like Lesley's coming to pay a visit," Sabrina observed. Samantha jerked back to the present with a snap.

She watched the late-model compact winding down the drive. Ignoring the flare of impossible jealousy, she set her features in casual lines.

"Sabrina, how well you look." Lesley's greeting was obviously tinged by surprise. "It's only been a week, and you look positively . . ." She hesitated, searching for a word.

"Radiant?" Sabrina suggested, and laughed. "I just had a baby, Lesley, not open-heart surgery."

"But to go through all that here, and without a doctor." She turned to Samantha. "I heard from Jake that you were marvelous and handled everything."

Samantha shrugged, uncomfortable at hearing Jake's praise from Lesley's lips. "It was nice of him to say so, but Sabrina did all the work."

"Well, having a baby is not a prospect I look forward to." Lesley shivered delicately. "I certainly intend to put it off as long as possible." Gliding over, she bent her head over the sleeping infant. "She is quite lovely, Sabrina. Very sweet."

"Would you like to hold her?" Samantha offered.

"Oh, no." Lesley stepped back. "I'm afraid I'm not very good with babies."

As she moved, Samantha caught the glint of the large square-cut diamond on her left hand. Lesley followed her gaze, and held out her hand. "You didn't know I was engaged, did you, Sabrina?"

"No." Sabrina cast a quick glance at her sister. "We hadn't heard."

"Well, you have been rather busy." She moved her fingers, enjoying the changing lights. "And we haven't made any formal announcement yet. We're planning a bit of a party for next week. As a matter of fact, I'm just on my way into town to begin shopping for my trousseau. Of course, I'll have to make a trip into New York for some proper clothes, but I'll just have to make do locally for the time being. We've set the wedding for the end of September." She smoothed her perfectly groomed hair with a well-manicured hand. "I could have done with a bit more time, but men have no idea how difficult things are to arrange properly." She smiled again. "Well, I must fly. I have so much to do. I do hope you'll be able to make it to the wedding, Samantha."

Sabrina glanced again at her sister. "Sam won't be here in September, Lesley."

"Oh, too bad." The regret in Lesley's voice was mild. Her mind had already run ahead to her wardrobe. She opened the door of the compact and slid behind the wheel. Lifting a slim arm in farewell, she drove away.

Rising, Sabrina took the sleeping Jennifer from her sister's arms and went into the house. When she returned, she sat on the arm of the rocker and laid her hand on Samantha's shoulder.

"I knew it was going to happen," Samantha murmured. "I just didn't want to be here when it did. I didn't think it would hurt this much. Oh, Bree." She looked up at her twin with helpless, swimming eyes. "What am I going to do?"

For the first time in their relationship, their situations were reversed, and Samantha was vulnerable, seeking comfort and advice.

"Sam, you can't go on like this. Why don't you talk to him?" Sabrina stroked the thick fall of her sister's hair. "Something is wrong here, and the two of you have to talk things out."

"No. I won't give him the opportunity to feel sorry for me."

"Pride can be a very cold companion," Sabrina murmured.

Samantha stood up. "I'm going back early, Bree. I can have everything arranged by the day after tomorrow, maybe even by tomorrow night."

"Sam, you can't run away from this."

"Just watch me."

"Mom and Dad won't be here for a few more days. They'll be disappointed."

"I'm sorry, I hate to miss them, but I can't handle this." Pausing, she repeated, the admission surprising her, "I *really* can't handle this."

"But, Sam . . ." Sabrina joined her at the porch rail. "You should at least talk to Jake. Don't you want to know how he feels? You can't just go flying off without speaking to him, without saying goodbye. Something's not right about all this. I've thought about the two of you. I've seen the way he looks at you."

Shaking her head, Samantha moved toward the door. "No, he hasn't shown his face since the baby was born, and Lesley Marshall has his ring on her finger. A diamond. He has what he wants."

Samantha spent the evening packing, while Shylock watched her in silent accusation from his habitual place in the center of her bed.

Once in bed, she spent most of the night staring at a moon-washed ceiling. When the first pale light of dawn crept into the room, she rose. The mauve shadows under her eyes were a sad tribute to the restless hours.

The house slept on, and she deserted it, making her way to the stables. She saddled her mount with quick, deft movements, then galloped over the faint mist of morning.

As the sky lightened, the air came to life with the sweet song of birds. Sadly, she listened to the song of the west, for she knew that the melody would linger forever in her heart. She watched the mountains transformed by the dawn. Ribbons of rose and gold melted into blue until the peaks were no longer silhouettes, but stood proud in the full glory of the sun. She stayed for a last look at the white-faced Herefords grazing on the short, coarse grass. She knew now that her love for this wild, free country was forever bound up with her love for Jake. In saying goodbye to one, she was saying goodbye to the other. Straightening her shoulders, she turned the little mare back to the Lazy L.

When she returned to the house, she greeted her sister with bright chatter, the meaningless words no disguise for sleep-starved eyes. Sabrina made no comment, and shortly disappeared into the bedroom to tend to the baby.

Alone, Samantha wandered aimlessly from window to window. Tonight, she thought, slipping her hands into the pockets of her jeans, I'll be on a plane. And tomorrow morning, all this will just be a dream.

"Morning, ma'am."

She whirled, nearly upsetting a vase of roses with the movement. Jake leaned against the door frame, legs crossed at the ankles, as if he had been watching for some time.

"What are you doing here?"

He took a few strides into the room. "Well,

now, I came to fetch you." This information was imparted in an irritatingly slow drawl.

"Fetch me? What are you talking about? I'm not a dog or a maverick calf to be fetched."

"Maverick calf sounds pretty close. You're always running off in the wrong direction." Reaching out, he took her arm. "Come on, we're going for a ride." His voice was pleasant, but the steel was there. She jerked away, angry with his arrogance, wary of his tone.

"I have no intention of going anywhere with you. Why don't you just go away and leave me alone?"

"Now, I can't do that, Sam," he returned in a reasonable tone. "We have some unfinished business to attend to. Your time's up."

The fire in her eyes flickered and died. "You can't be serious."

"I'm dead serious."

"What . . . what about Lesley?"

"She's not invited," he returned simply.

"I'm not going with you," she said, somewhere between terror and fury. "You can't make me."

Stopping, he looked down at her from his overpowering height. "Sure I can," he corrected with easy confidence. With a swift movement, he swung her over his shoulder. "See?" He walked effortlessly down the hall. "Nothing to it."

"Let me down!" Furious fists beat against his back. "This is crazy, it's illegal. I'll have you thrown in jail!"

"No kidding? Sam, you're scaring me to death."

He continued easily down the hall, as if he carried an empty sack, rather than an irate woman who was thumping against his back. Pausing, he touched the brim of his hat as Sabrina appeared in the bedroom doorway, the baby in her arms.

"Morning, Sabrina." His greeting was genial, and he cocked his head to get a better view of Jennifer. "She's a real beauty."

"Thank you, Jake. We certainly think so." She shifted the baby and smiled. "Are you two going out?"

"Thought we'd go for a little ride," Jake informed her. "We may be gone some time."

"It's a fine day for it, hardly a cloud in the sky."

"Bree." Samantha's voice was desperate. "Don't just stand there, *do* something." She pushed at the hair which hung over her face. "Don't you see what he's doing? He's kidnapping me. Call the police, call Dan." She continued to plead as Jake touched the brim of his hat once more and moved down the hall. "Bree, say something."

"Have a good time" was her sister's surprising response.

Samantha's mouth fell open in dumb astonishment. A stream of imaginative curses was hurled on Jake's unperturbed head as he took the reins of his mount from a grinning cowboy.

161

"Looks like you got yourself a real handful there, Jake."

"No more than I can handle," he countered, swinging into the saddle with Samantha still held over his shoulder. With a speed that defied his easygoing manner, he had her in front of him in the saddle, spurring the horse into a gallop, before she could think of escape.

"You're going to pay for this," Samantha promised, clutching the saddle horn to keep her balance. "You can't just run off with me this way!"

"I didn't see anybody try to stop me," Jake pointed out.

He followed the road for some time without decreasing his pace, then cut across an open field. At a small grove of trees, he reined in, gripping Samantha around the waist when she attempted to wiggle down.

"Now, don't do that, Sam," he warned in a friendly voice. "I'd just have to catch you, and I throw a mean lasso."

He slid from the chestnut, and before her feet could touch the ground, she was back over his shoulder. Without ceremony, she was dumped under the fragile, bending leaves of a willow while he towered over her, grinning with obvious enjoyment.

"You're going to be sorry," she predicted, smoldering with fury. "I'm going to . . ." The rest of her words slipped back down her throat as he dropped down next to her. "You — you can't do this, Jake. You're not the kind of man who forces himself on a woman."

"Who says?" Pushing her back on the soft grass, he covered her body with his.

Her body betrayed her with instant response. Her skin tingled as his mouth brushed over it. "You're not really going to do this."

"I told you once —" his mouth moved to her ear, and his words were warm and soft against it "— not to forget your own words. There are some things you just have to do."

His kiss was long and lingering.

When her mouth was free, she drew in a deep breath and spit out with all her strength, "What kind of man are you, to make love to one woman and plan to marry another?"

His eyes lazily narrowed. He propped himself on one elbow, his other arm pinning her down. Lifting his head from his elbow, he undid the top button of her blouse. "Suppose," he continued, moving down to the next button, "you tell me whom I'm supposed to marry."

His fingers trailed a slow line from her throat, down the smooth skin her open blouse revealed, and rested on the next button. The blood began to pound in her ears. His eyes alone held her still as he spread her blouse apart. Slowly, his fingers roamed up the warmth of her skin, moving with casual possession over her. Her eyes clouded with growing need as he explored.

"Tell me who I'm going to marry, Samantha." His body shifted again, molding to hers. His shirt was warm against her naked flesh.

"L-Lesley," she stammered.

"No." His mouth lowered to the curve of her throat, his tongue teasing the vulnerable skin.

She felt the waist of her jeans loosen under his hand. His finger pushed away the material and moved along her hip. With her last claim to lucidity, she pushed against his chest.

"Please stop."

"Now I just can't do that, Sam." His hands teased the curve of her hip, trailing back up to the side of her breast. "I've waited a good long time to get you where I want you."

"I'm not staying . . . Did you say you weren't marrying Lesley?"

He frowned down in consideration, winding her hair around his finger. "Seems to me I did mention that. I don't know why you're always piling your hair on top of your head when it looks so good spread all over."

"But she was wearing your ring."

"Not mine," Jake corrected, still concentrating on the hair around his fingers. "Your hair's gotten lighter these past few weeks, you haven't been wearing a hat. Les has a diamond, doesn't she? I told you once diamonds don't suit you. They're cold, and they don't have much imagination. But that's Les." He shrugged and began to move his mouth over her face again. "It doesn't seem to matter to Jim."

Valiantly, Samantha attempted to follow his words. Her head shook with the effort.

"Les is engaged to Jim Bailey. I'm sure you remember Jim Bailey, you spent enough time with him at the party."

"Yes, but . . ."

"No buts," he interrupted. "Les likes to have a couple of fish on the line, and when she got it through her head I wasn't in season, she netted Jim without a struggle."

"But I thought . . ."

"I know what you thought." He cut her off again and smiled. "Running away a few days early, weren't you?"

"I wasn't running. How did you know I was leaving?"

"Sabrina told me."

"Bree?" Samantha whispered. Bree did that?

"Yeah, yesterday. She came to see me while you were packing. I like this spot right here," he stated, planting his lips against the hollow of her throat. "I've had a devil of a time putting things in order since then, so I could take time for a honeymoon. Busy time of year for a cattleman."

"Honeymoon?" Her skin was trembling where his lips continued to taste.

"I've got a good foreman," he continued, as if thinking aloud. "I reckon he can manage things for a while. I could use another day or two. I had a nice long honeymoon in mind, someplace quiet." He brought his attention back to her stunned face. "You've never been to Bora Bora, have you?"

"Are you talking about getting your ranch in order so you can take time off to marry me?" She attempted to speak slowly and clearly while her emotions whirled like a summer tornado.

"Just being practical," he explained with a bland smile.

"Why you conceited, overbearing . . . Just what makes you think I'll marry you? You sit back and make all these plans and expect me to run off to Bora Bora with you like a passive little puppy. Of all the chauvinist —"

"How about Antarctica?" he suggested, willing to be reasonable. "Not too many people there, either."

"You're crazy. I never said I'd marry you. What makes you think . . ." Her tirade was cut off effectively as his mouth coaxed her silence. When he let her breathe, her voice had lost its strength. "That's not going to help you. I'm not in love with you."

"Seems to me I recall someone telling me she was a totally honest person." His gaze was disconcertingly direct. He held her chin, preventing her face from turning away. "You want to look at me and tell me that again? You've been fighting me all along, and I think I've just about used up my patience." His lips were teasing hers again, and his hands moved over her with more urgency. "Mmm, but you have a nice body. I can't take much more of this

166

waiting around. Six months is a long time, Sam. I've wanted you from the minute you stood there ordering Dan to have his man tend to the horses."

"Yes, you let me know very early what you wanted." She no longer struggled, but lay passive in his arms.

"Gave you something to think about. Of course, you didn't know I wanted you to be my wife, too. It was easy to tell you I wanted you, but a bit difficult to tell you I loved you. Sam, look at me." She shook her head, but the fingers on her chin tightened in authority. "Look at me." She obeyed, her lids opening to reveal eyes veiled with tears. "You stubborn little idiot. Listen carefully, I've never said this to another woman, and I've had to wait too long to say it to you. If you don't marry me soon, I'm going to lose my mind." His mouth took hers, spinning the world into nothing. Her arms flew around him as pain evaporated into unspeakable joy. "Samantha." He buried his face in the lushness of her hair. "It's been quite a race."

"I don't understand." She brought his face back to hers, needing to see the truth in his eyes. "Why didn't you tell me before?"

"I didn't think you'd believe that a man had nearly been knocked off his feet by a picture of a girl less than half his age, then had completely lost his balance when he saw the woman she'd become. If you hadn't been so wrapped up in

Sabrina those first few minutes, you'd have seen how a man looks when he gets hit by lightning."

"Just like that?" Stunned, she traced the angles of his face to assure herself she was not dreaming.

"Just like that," he agreed, bringing her palm to his lips. "Then, after I'd recovered a bit, I knew I had to work around your dedication to Sabrina until you'd figured out there was room in your life for someone else. Then you stood there telling me you were going back home as soon as the baby was born. I nearly strangled you." His fingers tightened on her hand as he brought his eyes back to hers. "How was I supposed to tell you that I loved you, that I wanted to marry you, wanted you to stay in Wyoming? The night of the party, in the kitchen, I made up my mind I wasn't letting you go, no matter what I had to do to keep you."

"But I never wanted to leave." She shook her head in brisk denial, as if he should have realized it all along. "It was just that I couldn't bear to see you married to Lesley."

"You know, things might have gotten even more complicated if Sabrina hadn't come by and laid things out for me. She's got a bit more of you in her than I had thought." Laughing, he lifted his face from hers. "She told me to sit down and listen. She'd never seen two people run around in circles so long and get nowhere."

"It's not like Bree to interfere."

"She interfered beautifully. First thing she did

was ask me what business I had getting engaged to Lesley. I must have stared at her like she'd lost her mind. After I managed to tell her I was definitely not engaged to Lesley, she let me have it with both barrels. Mixed with the buckshot was the information that you were miserable about going home, and that I was a fool for not seeing it myself. Then she folded her arms, stuck out her chin exactly like someone else has a habit of doing and asked me what the devil I intended to do about it."

Samantha stared up at him and shook her head in astonishment. "I wish I could have seen that."

He smiled and lowered his mouth. "Just look in the mirror sometime." Flesh met flesh with no barriers, and with a small sound of desperation he savaged her mouth. The hard lines of his chest pressed into her breasts. "Let me hear you say it, Samantha," he murmured, unable to resist the curve of her neck. "I need to hear you say it."

"I love you." Her mouth searched for his, her arms urging him closer. "I love you. I love you." Her lips found their objective, and her silence told him again.

"I need you, Samantha." His mouth and hands continued to seek, growing wilder, possessive, demanding. "I never knew I could need anyone the way I need you. I want you for myself for a while, no distractions, no complications, just you. We've got six months of loving to make up for. I'm going to keep you fully occupied for a very long time." Lifting his face, he smiled down at her, running his hand through the hair spread over the grass. "A very long time."

She smiled back, running her hands up his chest to circle his neck. "I intend to keep you occupied, as well. Your cows are going to get very lonely." Removing his hat, she tossed it carelessly aside, then turned back to him with raised brows. "Okay, cowboy." Her arms lifted to lock around his neck, fingers tangling possessively in his hair. "Start occupying."

"Yes, ma'am." With a polite nod, he lowered his mouth and followed orders.

The employees of Thorndike Press hope you have enjoyed this Large Print book. All our Thorndike and Wheeler Large Print titles are designed for easy reading, and all our books are made to last. Other Thorndike Press Large Print books are available at your library, through selected bookstores, or directly from us.

For information about titles, please call:

(800) 223-1244

or visit our Web site at:

www.gale.com/thorndike
www.gale.com/wheeler

To share your comments, please write:

Publisher
Thorndike Press
295 Kennedy Memorial Drive
Waterville, ME   04901